BLAZE OF GLORY

A Wildland Firefighter Romance

Blye Donovan

ISBN: 979-8-9867683-6-6
Imprint: Independently published.
Cover designed by CT Cover Creations.

For Barbara Ellington. There's immortality in fiction.

CONTENT WARNING

This book contains quite a bit of profanity because that's just how the characters speak. Also, Blaze is from California and likes to use the word, "hella." If you're not familiar with it, it can mean either "a lot" or "very" depending on the context.

He and Braylin also have the hots for each other and demanded multiple intimate scenes. Those happen on the page, so if you don't want to read them, feel free to skip or skim.

The story does contain mention of and talk about toxic relationships. I don't want to hinder anyone who might be in the process of healing, so be aware. But the bonus of this being a romance? You know there's a happy ending.

Lastly, I feel the need to make this disclaimer: (Clears throat) No animals were harmed in the making of this book . . . even those sporting antlers.

CHAPTER 1

Angel in the Sky

The scents of charred wood, smoke, and ash permeated the dry mountain air Noah "Blaze" Layne breathed while climbing to his lookout location. Towering trees filtered the June sun, but not enough to stop sweat beading on his face as he trekked. Summer for most people meant vacations spent lazing by the pool or on the beach, but for him, it meant time to go to work.

As a wildland firefighter, the smoky smells permeating the forest were familiar, but he kept note of the direction of the wind blowing into his nostrils. If it shifted, his hotshot crew's plans would have to change.

Acting as their scout, he headed for a high point overlooking the Lost Creek Fire. Southwest of his position, Blaze's crewmates worked on constructing an indirect fire line. Like all hand crews, they went where heavy equipment couldn't to create breaks that would slow the fire by lowering its intensity. Cutting line was hard and tedious work, but he didn't mind it. He actually preferred building line.

Today he'd been tapped for scout duty, though. Most enjoyed it as a break from the laborious process of digging, cutting, and raking a line in the earth to create a path with no fuel for the fire to consume, but he tended to get bored as a lookout.

Watching fire was hella less exciting than fighting it.

Despite being in excellent physical shape—a requirement for his job—the pace Blaze set had him huffing as he trudged up the sharp incline, past brush and sparse grasses covering the forest floor. The weight of his pack threatened to pull him backward and send him tumbling down the mountainside. He fought it with each step. Of course, the day he had lookout duty had to be on the steepest peak they'd scouted.

Above him, a mix of spruce and pine trees loomed, some as tall as buildings, but their lack of low branches provided little shade. Not that he wasn't used to the heat. Being a wildland firefighter meant working in heavy gear, Nomex flame-resistant clothing, and hot conditions.

Maybe it was a hazard of the job, but looking at the trees, all he saw was giant kindling. Wary of the dry conditions in the area, Blaze paused to listen. Birds sang while insects hummed—all normal sounds. No silence that spoke of fear.

The fire his crew fought remained far enough away.

While he continued to climb, a helicopter buzzed by on its way to drop retardant in front of the flames, and Blaze smiled. He loved the sound of its blades whacking the air because it meant help was coming. When the hotshot crews weren't the only ones on the fire, it was a good day.

Most didn't realize the goal of fighting a wildland fire wasn't to put it out but to *contain it* until it burned itself out. When it came to achieving that, crews like his were just one piece of the puzzle. Air assets like tankers and helicopters dropping water or retardant were another piece. Dozers and other ground equipment to move and clear downed timber and vegetation, which could act as fuels, rounded out the full picture.

Eyes on the sky and not his footing, Blaze's left

boot skidded over loose soil, and he slid several feet before he caught himself with the hand tool he carried, landing face-first and getting a mouthful of dust.

Coughing and spitting, he pushed to his feet. As if the smoke weren't bad enough, now he ate dirt. The grit coated his tongue and ground against his teeth. Shaking his head at himself, Blaze reached for a water bottle and swigged the liquid to clear his mouth. He'd have to pay more attention to the ground for the rest of his trek.

Storing his water back in his pack, Blaze continued climbing. The peak he sought rose around 11,000 feet above sea level, but his lungs were used to thin air. He'd grown up in central California with the Sierra Nevada Mountain Range as his backyard. The Rockies he traversed now were no different.

That was one thing he enjoyed about being a hotshot. Few people got to see as much of the country as he did . . . at least the fire-prone areas, anyway. His crew called California home. Well, *home* was relative. Sometimes Blaze felt rootless, whether from the nature of his job or some other source of dissatisfaction, but he wasn't entirely sure where *he* felt at home—other than with his crew.

One of the perks of working for the U.S. Forest Service was traveling wherever they were needed. In his five years as a wildland firefighter, he'd been all over the western United States.

At a grueling pace.

During fire season, his schedule consisted of fourteen-day rolls with two days off, and he didn't exactly work nine to five. It was normal to wake up before the sun and end the day hours after it set. Then, the cycle started all over again. Wildland firefighting wasn't so much a job as a lifestyle. If you didn't love it, you didn't do it. Especially when it made relationships difficult to maintain.

Blaze had learned that lesson his first summer out.

His chest throbbed with a dull ache, and he didn't know if it was from the memories that stirred to the surface or his meeting with the ground. His blue eyes pinched behind his mirrored safety glasses before he shoved away thoughts of his ex.

You're better off.

Noah got cheated on, but Blaze . . . Blaze didn't do relationships, so there was no chance of getting burned. Since his breakup with Sloane, he preferred sex with no entanglements, just fun on both sides. It was easier that way.

Plus, there was a draw to playing the field. He liked the challenge. Like fighting fires, Blaze craved that stimulation. He glanced up the slope in a better head space now.

Almost there. Another few minutes and he'd reach his vantage point.

When he crested the top of the peak, Blaze set down his McLeod—a combination hoe and rake tool—and leaned against it to catch his breath. Sweat pooled at his temples. Underneath the weight of his ash-smeared yellow helmet, his blonde hair matted to his scalp with perspiration. The safety helmet had been clean once, but the layer of smut gave testament to the amount of time he'd had it. He could hardly be called a shiny rookie anymore.

Proud of that fact, Blaze lifted his binoculars and gazed across the landscape, watching the bright swath of orange eat up all the dry timber and vegetation in its path.

Hungry Beast.

The near-drought conditions Colorado had been experiencing meant the normally dry mountainside was parched. After a group of hikers failed to extinguish a campfire properly, it turned into a fast-moving, acre-consuming blaze.

The cloud of smoke it created dampened the glow of the mid-morning sun but did little to stave off its heat. Today, the temperature would reach the mid-90s.

Straightening, Blaze secured the McLeod tool to his pack. He'd made note of the main burn, but his focus shifted to scanning for other hazards, like spot fires. Those tended to pop up when the wind carried flaming sparks into vegetation across the line. So far, he didn't see anything that would endanger his crewmates. But he knew how fickle Mother Nature could be and how quickly things could turn.

Several thousand feet below his vantage point, a valley stretched out with a tiny trickle of dark blue water snaking to the horizon.

Gorgeous.

But as he admired the view, Blaze kept one eye on the fire. When he felt the wind shift direction, his pulse spiked. Pulling out his weather meter, he checked the wind speed. The number turned into a pit in his stomach. With an eye on the blaze, he calculated the risk.

Not good.

Gripping the transceiver attached to his pack, he radioed his supervisor about the change in conditions. His crew had been digging a line south of the fire, but now the wind made that line irrelevant. Instead, the fire raced across the mountain—right for Blaze.

Watching the wind drive embers into the tree-tops momentarily froze him. "Well, fuck."

The fire was crowning, and the head picked up speed as it roared in his direction. He stood in the green—the fuel zone. As in the literal line of fire where dry trees, shrubs, and grasses waited to feed the damned thing.

Today just got a bit more exciting.

Blaze blinked and sprang into action. His heart sped with adrenaline as he considered his options. The rapid spread of the fire's perimeter would cut off his first planned escape, which meant going with option number two—the more treacherous route. Swallowing to wet his dry throat, he radioed the update and told his boss his next move.

"Copy, Blaze. Stay alert and be smart." The radio crackled before Charlie added, "Avoid entrapment. We'll shift the line down here. Just make it to us."

"That's the plan, Cap," Blaze answered with his trademark swagger, but in all reality, he sweated bullets. He hoped like hell he'd be able to make it out of this 'watch-out situation'. There were 18 of those every wildland firefighter knew by heart, and he happened to be in one.

Wind increases and/or changes direction. Fuck yeah, it changed direction.

Wasting no more time, Blaze started heading downhill—fast. He let his pack act as a counterbalance as he tried not to tumble his way to the bottom. Pebbles slid along with him, and he prayed he wouldn't twist an ankle on them.

That's the last thing I need.

He made good progress until his boot caught in a tree root, tripping him. As if in slow-motion, he watched the gravel in front of him slide. Then his pack shifted forward, throwing off his balance. Time fast-forwarded, and he lost the battle to stay upright. An invisible weight pulled him into a somersault, rolling him several painful feet before he took a header into a tree, and the world faded to black.

* * *

"I need a drop along the tree line." Braylin's headset squawked with the instruction from her ground contact as she positioned the helicopter to do as he asked.

"Four Nin-er November copies," she answered using her call sign. Familiar static filled her ears as she turned her mic on again. She'd been a pilot for eight years, the majority of those with the military. "Lining up for the drop."

The bright orange bucket suspended one hundred and fifty feet below the aircraft swung as she turned, but she steadied it with the skills she'd gained the last three years as an aerial firefighter.

A cloud of smoke filled the air, and she stayed outside its grasp. The fire had grown over the short time it had taken for her to refill her bucket of water. The 200 gallons she carried weren't likely to do much against the blaze tearing across the mountainside, but that wouldn't stop her from trying. With another glance at her target, Braylin pushed the release button.

Water away.

She leaned her head into the side window, her white helmet kissing the glass as she watched the bucket empty its contents a little behind where she'd wanted it to. "Damn wind."

It pushed the water further into the tree line than she would've liked. Nothing she could do about it but refill and attack the line again.

With a sigh, she pulled out of the drop, turning parallel to the mountainside to head back down to the water source she'd been filling from. The Forest Service had a tank set up in a nearby valley that wouldn't take her long to reach, but as she started to fly away, a spot of yellow among the trees caught her eye. There shouldn't be a shot crew down there, not when the flames had nearly reached that location.

Braylin twisted her head, and a frown line marred her forehead. That was most definitely a damned yellow helmet and shirt.

This guy must have a death wish.

With the intent to get in touch with whoever this idiot was, she reached out to her ground contact again. "Davis, this is Four Nin-er November requesting relay. I've got eyes on a hotshot less than a quarter mile from the drop zone, directly east of the fire."

A long pause followed her request for the hotshot's radio frequency, and she orbited right to circle around and keep him in her sights. It didn't look like he'd moved since she'd last laid eyes on him.

That's a bad sign.

Waiting made her skin feel tight. She blew out a breath to settle her building anxiety. The air ruffled the sprigs of brown hair that had escaped from underneath her helmet, and she shoved them back in.

After what felt like an eternity, Davis

responded, "Copy, Four Nin-er November, that area should be clear." *No shit.* She wasn't one to roll her eyes—okay, yes, she was—but this situation ratcheted up her nerves. "He's got to be crew three. The Sierra Hotshots are using frequency one-two-one point nine-five-zero."

Braylin hoped whoever this guy was, he had a radio as she opened communications. "Sierra Hotshot, this is helicopter Four Nin-er November. Be advised you are in immediate danger," she paused to let that sink in before adding, "I repeat, immediate danger. The fire is less than a quarter mile from your location. Please respond."

When she got no response and still no movement, Braylin tried again, repeating her message. After her third try met with only silence, she had to acknowledge the hotshot didn't have a radio or—worse—he was unable to answer. Either reality meant they needed a rescue asset. Her stomach had snarled into a ball of stress as she contacted Davis again and radioed the situation.

Braylin continued to orbit while her ground contact broke the news. *She* was the closest rescue asset. Her eyes searched for a landing zone, but with the trees and the incline, she couldn't find one. The only way to get this guy out would be from the ground, and that option would take too long for how fast the fire moved unless . . . A crazy idea formed, but the hotshot had to be conscious for it to work.

* * *

Blaze woke with a groan, blinking up at branches shrouded in a smoky haze. He must be on a fire. Confused, he sat up, but the new position brought on a wave of nausea. His head felt like a vice clamped around it, so he reached to remove his helmet and relieve some of the pressure.

What the hell happened?

Over the ringing in his ears, a woman's voice penetrated his jumbled thoughts. ". . . immediate danger. I need you to climb in the bucket."

It took him longer than it should have to realize the voice came from his radio. She kept repeating 'immediate danger', and the memory of running from the fire flooded back in.

How long was I out?

Probably too long to make it down the mountain now. Carefully, so as not to jostle his pounding head, Blaze pushed to his feet. Had he given himself a concussion? He'd had training in emergency medical services to support his crew. They often worked remotely where access to paramedics wasn't readily available, and he liked being prepared.

The woman spoke again, and he looked toward the noise radiating above him. A white and blue helicopter hovered carrying a pumpkin. He frowned at it as her voice floated around him, discernible even over the sound of the rotor wash. It was almost melodic, the tone rising and falling like the notes of a song. As he stared, the pumpkin lowered to the ground a few feet below his position.

No, not an actual pumpkin. The bucket. His thoughts were a little sluggish, but what she kept telling him finally penetrated. She wanted him to climb into that thing.

You got to be kidding me.

Blaze stared at the small orange vessel. It couldn't be much more than three feet in diameter and around the same in height. He wasn't even sure he would fit with the metal support bars crossing the top of it. At six feet two, the bucket looked like a child's toy, and some crazy lady wanted to hoist him thousands of feet into the air with it?

No fucking way.

But even as his thoughts rebelled against that option, he heard the roar of the fire he couldn't outrun. A glance to his right and his breath rushed out in fear. The hungry beast raged much too close, devouring all the fuel in its path.

"Climb in the bucket, now!" The panic in the woman's voice put his feet in motion.

Blaze gripped the support bars and stepped into the water bucket. His other foot had barely landed inside when he felt it jerk as she lifted him off the ground. He held onto the suspension line to keep from falling out. The swinging motion didn't help his nausea or his head, but it was still the better option.

While the chopper flew away from the fire, a wave of shock bowled over him, and Blaze watched with wide eyes as it consumed the spot he'd been standing in moments before. Had he *not* gotten into the bucket, the flames would've engulfed him.

In a daze of disbelief, he lifted his transceiver to his mouth and said the only words he could muster, "Thank you."

Whoever she was, this woman had just become his angel in the sky.

CHAPTER 2

No Good Deed

Paperwork.

That's what her improvised rescue would cost her. After the adrenaline of extricating the hotshot wore off, dread at the realization twisted in Braylin's gut, and she groaned. There was little she hated more than paperwork, and now she would have to write a safety report on the incident. Why had the damned fool been there in the first place? The second she set him down, she planned to find out, which she hoped to do at the first opportunity.

As she flew away from the fire, Braylin's eyes scanned for a suitable spot to land. If the powers that be had any mercy left, she'd find wherever the hotshots were camped. Not sure what condition her passenger was in, she'd already requested medical assistance, but she still needed to give the paramedics her location once they set down.

At least he'd seemed coherent enough to thank her. She hadn't responded, but now that Braylin thought about it, she ought to make sure he hadn't fallen out. Grumbling about the amount of paperwork *that* might cost her, she keyed her radio. "Hey, Sierra. You still with me down there?"

"Sure am, angel." *Angel? Really?* Braylin scowled, but before she could complain about the name, he asked, "Any chance you might set me on the ground soon? My head's not loving this bucket flight."

Humor colored the statement, but it didn't hide the fact he sounded like he was going to be sick. "Do NOT hurl in my bucket."

"Roger." A gulp. "But no promises." The transmission broke before he added with a strained plea, "You might want to land us sooner than later."

Oh, for fuck's sak—There! A valley opened up below them, and Braylin sighed in relief. Hosing vomit out of the water bucket would have topped the paperwork she had to do. "Hold it in, Sierra. You'll be on the ground in less than a minute."

"Blaze."

"What? Where?" *Shit!* Her head swiveled, looking out the windows of the aircraft for a new fire. Taupe mountainsides with an all too familiar shade of army-green trees swept out from the valley on either side of them. She didn't see any smoke.

"No"—he chuckled weakly—"that's my name. Blaze."

What kind of ridiculous name is Blaze?

"What's yours, angel?" Why did his voice suddenly sound seductive? Its rasp sent a wave of heat rolling over her, and Braylin blinked in surprise before she gave herself a mental punch in the boob.

No matter what he sounds like, you're still pissed at this idiot.

When she didn't respond, he asked again, "Angel?"

"Brace yourself," Braylin warned.

She might've set the bucket down a little faster than necessary, but she was ready to unload her unwanted passenger.

* * *

Blaze climbed out of the bucket on shaky legs once the helicopter landed a few feet away. He bent over with his hands on the tops of his knees, swallowing down the contents of his stomach that threatened to come back up from the dizziness racking his senses. Cursing, he closed his eyes, but when that made the spinning more intense, he popped them open again. As he focused on his breathing, the whirring of the blades slowly faded as they came to a stop.

Forcing himself to stand up straight, Blaze grabbed onto the suspension line of the bucket for balance. Slower than he would've liked, the world settled, and then a gorgeous brunette walked toward him.

The top of her milk chocolate hair glinted in the sun, teasing him with hints of chestnut. A few strands had escaped her ponytail and framed her heart-shaped face. She had full lips and a straight, narrow nose below eyes hidden behind a pair of mirrored shades. His fingers twitched with the urge to remove them and discover what color they'd be.

Despite the lingering nausea, his face broke into a grin. His angel was smokin' hot, and he could think of multiple ways he'd like to repay her for saving his life.

She stopped a couple of feet away and propped her hands on the swell of her hips. The position pulled in the baggy material of her green flight suit, showcasing her slim waist.

"Angel." Blaze extended a hand, but she merely glanced at it before her sultry mouth turned down in a scowl.

"What the hell were you doing in that location?"

Blaze raised an eyebrow and dropped his hand when it became clear she had no intention of shaking it. The woman was pissed at him, though he didn't know why. "Scouting." He couldn't help a cocky grin as he added, "You know, my job?" He resisted the temptation to call her sweet thing— barely. Her prickliness made him want to test out those spikes because she packed heat, and he bet it'd be explosive in bed.

She actually scoffed, and the fingers on her hips started tapping as she shot back, "You're not a very good lookout if you let the fire get that close to you."

Nice one, angel. She must've expected that to piss him off because she gave him such an arch, superior look. Unfazed, he started to laugh, but an arrow of pain sliced through his head, turning the laughter into a groan as he closed his eyes and put a hand to his temple. "Fuck."

"Hey, you're looking kind of green. Maybe you

should sit down." Her voice grew louder on the last statement as if she'd moved closer.

Blaze *felt* a little green as another wave of nausea followed the headache. When a hand landed on his arm, his eyes flew open, catching on the black name tag attached to her suit. Not that he was looking at her chest or anything. Yeah, he totally was. *Whitney.* Pretty name.

"Just sit. The EMTs are on their way." She practically forced him onto the ground, so Blaze sat, his knees up, his back touching the bucket.

To his surprise, she sat beside him. The soft scents of lavender and vanilla reached his nose, and a very uninjured part of him took notice. *Interesting.*

He swallowed, then took a few deep breaths. When he felt sure his stomach had settled, he explained, "I lost my footing, tumbled I-don't-know-how-many feet until my head hit a tree and stopped my fall. I guess I blacked out because I woke up to you telling me to get in the bucket."

She sighed heavily as if his explanation had put an extra weight on *her* shoulders. "You might have a concussion." A pause then mumbling that sounded like, "And I have *more* paperwork."

He concurred and smiled through the pain. Paperwork wasn't something he enjoyed either.

"So . . . *Whitney*?"

She sat with her legs crossed under her, picking at blades of grass. When he spoke, her eyes met his and narrowed. "Yep."

He wondered if he should offer a hand again, then thought better of it. "I'm Noah, but everyone calls me Blaze."

"What's with the nickname?" Her smirk told him she thought it was the most ridiculous thing she'd ever heard.

A self-deprecating chuckle burst from his lips. It *was* ridiculous because it sounded cool, while in reality, it just showcased another of his fuckups. "How about I tell you when you haven't already witnessed enough of my humiliation for one day."

She half scoffed, half snorted. "At least you didn't throw up in the bucket."

He hadn't. But he'd been damned close to doing so. Blaze squeezed the back of his neck and shrugged it off. "Yeah, at least there's that."

* * *

Braylin leaned against the helicopter with her arms crossed over her chest as the paramedics looked Blaze over. She was too far away to hear the conversation, but she didn't miss the flash of his movie-star smile. All gleaming white teeth and manly creases. The soot on his face only made them more pronounced. When her stomach responded with a fluttering sensation, she scowled in his direction.

Why did he have to be so damn good-looking?

Even underneath all the grime, he belonged on the cover of a surfing magazine. Wavy, beach-blonde hair, blue eyes that managed to shine like a clear sky despite the obvious pain in his head, and the biceps she'd felt when she'd put her hand on his arm . . . she could imagine the rest of him was just as sculpted. Why couldn't she have rescued some bearded, balding, middle-aged hotshot with all the comeliness of a sack of grain? *So* unfair.

She really wanted to dislike Blaze, and her body's obvious physical reaction did not help with that effort. Yes, she was attracted. She could admit it, but it didn't change the fact that she didn't get involved with guys she worked with. One colossal mistake was enough to sear that lesson into her very bones.

Remembering it, Braylin straightened, clutching her middle as her insides tied themselves into solid knots.

Right. She knew better than to cross that line

again.

Blowing out a breath, she sent the sour memories away with the dispelled air. Relaxing enough to take up her previous position against the side of the aircraft, Braylin glared in Blaze's direction. The struggle came because he'd made her feel sorry for him. She'd nearly winced in sympathy when he'd frozen, his eyes shut so tightly it pinched his whole face against the pain in his head. Then he'd turned that sickly peaked color and—

I should've let him puke in the bucket.

If she had, it'd be much easier to hate him right now. Surely, cleaning up vomit would've squashed any attraction she felt.

Grumbling about it under her breath, she wondered how much longer the EMTs would take. At this rate, she'd be typing up the incident long after her shift had ended. The report she had to write seemed like punishment for her good deed, so she may as well lay the blame on him.

Yep. There. Braylin nodded. She just had to focus on the hours she'd spend writing up the rescue when Blaze next tried to shoot her that smile of his.

The cocky bastard.

He gave off total playboy vibes. She knew the

type. The kind of guy who had a lot of dates and not a lot of relationships. Well, she wasn't about to be another name in his little black book. Braylin snorted. Not that he even *knew* her name. The tag on her flight suit only had her last name; when he'd mentioned it, she hadn't bothered correcting him. But it didn't matter. She had no plans to see him again once this was done.

Finally, the paramedics started packing up their medical bags, and Blaze stood, glancing in her direction. She inclined her head, and he started toward her.

When he stopped in front of her, his height kept the sun from her eyes. Her fingers twitched with the temptation to remove her shades and get a better look at him. But she didn't. She liked the shield they gave her.

Behind her mirrored lenses, her eyes drank in the defined cheekbones, the strong jawline covered in blonde stubble—both now revealed after the EMTs had wiped his face clean. His bone structure was sharp where his lips, his hair were all soft. He quirked an eyebrow, waiting for her to say something. She *had* called him over here. Then she'd gotten distracted, drooling over the angles of his face.

Clearing the lust from her brain, Braylin

asked, "So what's your damage?"

"A mild concussion. They're going to drive me back to where my crew's spiked out," he paused for a beat, then that damned Hollywood grin split his face. "Unless you want to keep an eye on me for the next twenty-four hours?"

So damn cocky.

Something stirred low in her belly, and she told herself it was only anger. "As I have hours of work to do yet—thanks to you—I'm afraid I have to pass."

"I thought you might say that." He shrugged and gestured behind him. "Lana offered to monitor me, but I'll be with my crewmates in camp. No need to take up anyone else's time."

A coil of something suspiciously like jealousy wrapped around her chest, and she shifted slightly to see who he'd gestured to. Sure enough, a pretty blonde paramedic stared in their direction. Braylin guessed she shouldn't be surprised he'd charmed someone else. The man oozed it like pheromones.

Annoyed at herself, Braylin opened her mouth, and her voice came out harsher than necessary. "I need a way to contact you in case I have questions for the report I have to write."

Blaze met her demand with an easy smile

before rattling off a cell number. "You call that anytime." He winked at her, and then his voice dropped to the seductive tone she'd heard over the radio. "Especially if you change your mind."

"I won't." The words tumbled out through her honed preservation instinct as the warmth of the fire he'd started licked toward her core. Her eyes locked with his, and she knew she had an unfair advantage since he couldn't see hers. His heated the longer she stared, making her wonder . . .

Her eyes dropped to his lips, but then Lana called his name. Blaze gave Braylin one last smoldering look before he turned and walked away.

That's for the best.

Despite what she told herself, a part of her regretted not stopping him. For what . . . she didn't know.

CHAPTER 3

A Blessing or a Curse

Braylin didn't have enough coffee in her system to get through this meeting. She drained the last of the dark brew from her mug and set it on the wood-veneered conference table. Once her boss had gotten word of her rescue effort yesterday, he'd called for an after-action review—the dreaded A.A.R.—with the whole crew. Because of that, she'd dragged her butt to the company's headquarters.

The office building stood just outside Leif Aero's hangar, where assets were parked when not out on a contract. She'd been in the conference room a handful of times over her three years with the company—none of them good. Typically, she tried to avoid the modern glass-fronted building as much as possible, preferring to stay away from the "head shed," as she and the other pilots liked to call the decision-makers at Leif Aero. She'd take the fading metal hangar or the cockpit over a boardroom any day.

Two other company pilots had decided to join, though why they'd want to sit through this at seven in the morning was beyond her. She felt bad for her crew chief and the three maintenance guys he'd roped into attending. The company safety officer ran the A.A.R., and he had a voice that settled into a monotone of endless unintelligible words as he droned on. Braylin had almost nodded off twice from its lull. Well, from that and the lack of sleep she'd gotten the night before after waking up from some very . . . *disturbing* dreams.

Frown lines creased her forehead as she remembered every vivid detail of those dreams. The ones where she and Blaze were busy creating their own inferno. She squeezed her legs together as the images made the spot low in her belly tighten into a coil that vibrated with enough tension to spring free from the pressure alone. Her hazel eyes glazed over as she stared, unseeing, at the projector screen on the wall across the meeting room. Various aircraft accidents flashed on the screen, but they were a blur of dull colors she couldn't make out as she debated with herself.

The problem was obvious. It had been too long since she'd had sex. Her last relationship ended nearly six months ago, and until now, she hadn't been interested in a new one. Not that she wanted a relationship with that playboy. The idea he'd even be capable of one made her scoff. She knew how *that* would end, and the things her body wanted from him were *not* going to happen, even if her dreams said otherwise. Besides, she'd likely never see Blaze again.

All she needed was a relaxing bath and a good night's sleep . . . *and* a session with B.O.B. Her vibrator would solve this . . . this pent-up sexual tension because that's *all* her response to Blaze was. Relief at her resolution loosened the coil in Braylin's belly, and she gave a sharp nod of reassurance.

"You agree, Whitney? That's excellent."

At hearing her last name, Braylin's head snapped to Mike, the safety officer.

What?

She'd utterly zoned him out and had no idea what he was talking about. In her lap, her hands twisted with anxiety while she schooled her face into a bland expression to cover the surprise she'd first thrown his way.

Shit, what did I just agree to?

Everyone in the room swiveled to stare at her with various levels of disbelief, and she had a sinking feeling in her stomach that whatever it was, she wouldn't like it. Mike gave her an encouraging smile. *Fuck. Shit. Damn.*

Braylin smiled back and hoped it didn't look as fake as it felt. "Yes, absolutely." *Now, please tell me what the hell we're talking about.*

But it wasn't Mike who spoke next. Her boss leaned forward in his chair and slapped his hands together, addressing the entire room. "Well, that settles it then."

Settles what? Inside, Braylin screamed in near panic.

"Whitney will test out the concept with the hotshot she saved, and we'll build the training around her experiences." Dale turned to her, his dour face set in hard lines, and all the coffee she'd drunk became a balloon filled with lead in her stomach as he said, "I'll expect weekly reports on your progress. You're off active fires until this is ironed out. Understood?"

She gulped and sucked in a sharp breath, hoping it wasn't as audible as it sounded in her ears. No, that was most definitely *not* understood.

They wanted her to do *what*, exactly? And with Blaze? The balloon in her stomach popped, exploding into a frenzy of fireworks that proceeded to ping around her insides.

"Sir," she started, but he'd already risen from the table. The rest of the room followed suit, and a cacophony of people's voices mixed with the noise of rolling chairs sliding into the table. It drummed in her head as she stared at the spot Dale had been. This was bad. Very bad.

A hand clamped on her shoulder, and she jumped. "Hey, Whit. You okay? Seem a little out of it." Her crew chief's concerned brown eyes looked her over. "I'm surprised you agreed to that." Roger jerked a finger toward Mike, who chatted with one of the other pilots.

Braylin climbed out of her chair and grabbed Roger's arm. "I couldn't sleep and missed most of what was said." She lowered her voice. "Please tell me what I've signed up for." With a desperate squeeze of his arm, her eyes begged him to tell her it wasn't as bad as she feared. Roger looked out for her when it came to maintenance issues, and she returned the favor with anything she caught wind of from the pilot side of the house.

His gaze widened, and he spoke in a low rumble accented by his years of growing up in

New York, "You don't know?"

All she could do was shake her head.

"The Forest Service is demanding a response to the incident. That was why the boss wanted an A.A.R. His balls were in a vice." Braylin cringed when that unpleasant image sprang to her mind. "They want you cross-training with that hotshot. Eyes in the sky talking to eyes on the ground to better understand each other's perspective on a fire." Roger shrugged his broad shoulders. At forty-five, he was like the beefy older brother she'd never had. Mischief sparkled in his eyes before he added, "You know, a"—he made air quotes with his fingers—"'lessons learned' and 'best way forward' kind of thing."

"Dammit," she grumbled under her breath. Carrying a hotshot in the water bucket was unconventional. She'd known it would lead to safety questions, but she hadn't imagined this. Lessons learned meant reports and paperwork— her least favorite things.

Roger heard her and chuckled. "Yeah, good luck."

She released Roger's arm and scowled. "Don't."

He just shook his head with a smile and left. Braylin didn't move from her spot as if that could stop her from having to train with Blaze. Her brain raced while her body stood frozen. Maybe there was a way out of this. Surely, someone better qualified than her should be leading this endeavor.

Yes! She just needed to talk another pilot into taking over for her . . . but even as she explored that idea, her shoulders fell. Dale had already assigned her the task. She'd look like a shitbag if she pawned it off on someone else now. *Damn.*

How was she going to train with Blaze when one—she didn't like him—and two—she wanted to jump his bones? Braylin's thoughts sped with potential solutions to her hotshot problem, but each one she tested came up short . . . or veered in a dangerous direction. The fact she'd even considered having sex with Blaze to scratch her itch meant she'd let this get out of control. That earned her a double mental punch in the boob.

B.O.B. and I are definitely having a date tonight.

The only upside she could see was that Blaze would likely be down for a few days with his head injury, which gave her time to cool off and come up with a better plan. Maybe she'd get lucky, and his superintendent wouldn't agree to the training. A seed of hope bloomed in her chest at the thought. She'd nurture the hell out of that little guy and pray for the best.

Seeing Mike standing alone, Braylin pushed her shoulders back and sucked it up. If she didn't end up getting out of this, she wanted to be prepared. Grumbling about playboy hotshots under her breath, she headed for the safety officer to discuss his ideas for this hare-brained scheme.

* * *

Blaze had been given two days off due to his injury. He could've gone into the nearest town and enjoyed himself, but the desire to do so hadn't been there. Instead, he'd spent the last day and a half alternately sleeping—who knew he'd been so damned tired?—and thinking about Whitney, his grumpy angel. As he lay in his tent, staring up at a spot in the green canvas where the stitching had come loose, he wished he'd taken *her* number since she didn't seem inclined to call *his*.

That was a first for Blaze. Not for Noah, who'd had his share of rejections before Sloane, but *Blaze* didn't strike out. Maybe that's why Whitney lingered in his thoughts—she hadn't fallen for his charm. She'd been cold, harsh, and clearly annoyed with him. And *that* intrigued the hell out of him. Something had to be wrong with his head.

Probably knocked a few screws loose ramming it into a tree. Although her pretty face, hot body, and take-no-shit attitude might have something to do with the reason she lingered in his thoughts, too.

He'd like to see what she could do in the sack with all that fire she seemed to be fueled with. His eyes closed as his brain summoned a fantasy he'd been nurturing since he'd first laid eyes on the feisty brunette. It started with him showing up at her hotel room and ended with her legs wrapped around his waist in the shower, the hot water sluicing over her pert breasts as her back arched against the tiles.

A loud slam outside his tent pulled Blaze from his fantasy. He opened his eyes with a groan at the interruption. But it was for the best. He hadn't spent so much time thinking about a woman since Sloane.

The headache he couldn't seem to get rid of throbbed behind his eyes at the thought of the woman who'd stomped all over his heart. It had been five years, and an ember of anger still smoldered deep in his chest over how she'd treated him.

At least Whitney looked nothing like *her*. Sloane had been a petite, busty blonde with brown doe eyes that had done a number on him. They'd been her weapons, manipulating him with tears whenever it suited her. The ember in his chest burned a little hotter at the memories.

Whitney was Sloane's physical opposite. She had a tall, slim build and light brown hair. He only wished he'd seen her eyes. Would they be blue, brown, or something even more interesting like hazel? The sparks from old wounds died down as he pictured his angel's eyes behind those mirrored shades she'd worn.

Damn, he had it bad. Mooning over a woman's possible eye color.

Blaze sat up and ran his hands down his face. They scratched against the day-old scruff he hadn't bothered to shave. Too much time off was the problem. He needed to do something to clear his head. Get back on the line, feel the heat of a fire raging at his back as he and his crewmates fought against time to stop it. That's the rush he needed . . . well, if he couldn't have his angel.

Of its own accord his hand reached toward his phone to check for the tenth time in the last few hours.

Still no messages from her.

With a sigh, Blaze tossed it onto his sleep sack and got to his feet. He'd go for a walk and—his stomach rumbled—maybe hunt down some grub.

Opening the tent flap sent a smoke-filled haze spilling in. The air where the crew had spiked out a camp was heavy with it. They'd likely have to move if the wind kept sending it in their direction.

Blaze stepped outside and glanced up. A thick, smoky cloud that stretched the width of the sky muted the afternoon sun's rays. Seeing it made him long to be back on the ridge, putting in the work with his crew.

Soon.

Lowering his gaze, he glanced around the camp. It was quiet in the middle of the afternoon, with only a few support personnel wandering around. His crewmates had left at dawn. Their empty tents flapped in the breeze blowing past the trailers with the showers and toilets. Blaze didn't mind roughing it, but the powers-to-be running this fire had provided them with catered meals and real bathrooms. It was more like glamping than anything. Hoping there'd be something for lunch, he headed for the food tent.

He'd only gone a few steps when the sound of his name stopped him mid-stride. "Blaze!"

He turned to see who'd yelled it and found his supervisor, Charlie, headed in his direction. "Hey, Cap," Blaze greeted him when he approached, surprise coloring his voice. "How come you're not out with the crew?"

Charlie breathed hard like he'd just run down the mountain. "I was," he paused to pull in a breath. "But I got a call." He wiped the sweat from his face, smearing a line through the grime that came from working under falling ash. "We're moving."

Disappointment clanged through Blaze. A part of him had hoped he'd get the chance to see Whitney again, but if they were on to a new fire, that possibility dwindled. "Oh, okay. Where are we headed?"

"You're not coming."

Righteous anger burned its way up Blaze's throat. Suddenly, he was sixteen again and his coach benched him for a minor injury. "What the hell, Cap! You know I'm fine. I've already been cleared to start back to work tomorrow."

Charlie bent over and held up a hand. "Damn smoke," he grumbled. After a few deep inhales, he looked up at Blaze. "This is coming from Supe. They tagged you for some kind of training to do with your accident."

What? A puzzled frown tugged on Blaze's lips at the mention of his crew's superintendent. "What kind of training?" He didn't like the idea of being pulled away from his crewmates, but he *had* fucked up. And if he hadn't been rescued . . . He guessed this was the price he had to pay.

Charlie finally straightened, his breathing a little less labored. "Cross-training with an air asset. Forest Service wants better lines of communication between air and ground to prevent the need for things like bucket rides."

His captain lifted an eyebrow, and Blaze winced. He'd really rather not repeat *that* experience. "So, who drew the short straw?" He figured whoever his air asset was, they'd be about as excited for cross-training as he was if it meant getting pulled from fighting fire.

"Leif Aero. And I think the same pilot that rescued you."

Blaze's heart skipped a beat. *No shit?*

Charlie removed his helmet and ran a hand through his matted red hair. "Supe said they'd be calling you. Just sit tight until then."

Blaze tried to hold in the grin, but it still colored his response, "All right." He cleared his throat, schooling his features. It wouldn't bode well if Cap thought he was happy about leaving the crew. "Thanks for letting me know."

Charlie took a step toward him and clasped Blaze's shoulder. "Keep me updated. I want you back with us as soon as possible."

"Same, Cap. Same." *Liar*. Right now, all he could think about was seeing his angel again.

Charlie nodded and released him. As his captain walked away, a grin spread across Blaze's face. His outlook had improved considerably at this turn of events.

When his phone started ringing, he forgot his hunger and the walk he'd planned to take. Adrenaline surged through his veins, and Blaze dove for the tent flap. He lifted it and stalled like an engine before it took a nosedive.

He heard his phone, but he didn't see it.

Blaze fell to his knees and ran his hands over his sleeping bag, searching for the rectangle of plastic hidden within its folds. His fingers brushed the case, and he sat back on his feet in relief.

When he lifted the phone, he noted the unknown number that flashed on the screen. Excitement danced down his spine. "Layne," he answered.

"Blaze?"

At the sound of his angel's voice, Blaze sank down onto his sleep sack and smiled widely at nothing. "Angel. I knew you couldn't stay away," he teased, hoping to get a rise out of her.

She didn't disappoint. "Hardly." He pictured

the eye-roll he heard in her tone. "Do you have a minute?"

Blaze chuckled and poked the bear. "Sweet thing, we're going to need longer than a minute."

CHAPTER 4

Lessons Learned

Braylin was going to murder him. And she didn't even care if it looked like an accident or not. Going to prison would be worth it if it meant ridding her of Blaze fucking Layne. It only took her three days to reach her limit. Three days of his cocky bullshit, and she was ready to be sentenced. She'd gladly take twenty-five to life just to be free from him.

"Dammit, Blaze! I told you not to try that! Do you ever listen?" Even though they were training, and the scenario wasn't real, he'd just climbed into the green, directly under her dropping zone. The 'fire' they fought to stop was now too close to his position.

"Typical, just typical," she muttered. It had been a long and frustrating three days.

Every situation they'd tested in the simulator so far had ended in either entrapment for Blaze or a loss of visual flight rules for her. Either he got caught in the fire and burned to a crisp, or she got stuck in the smoke and couldn't tell up from down, leading her to crash. Today marked their first day of training in the real world, and it wasn't going much better.

Her radio in the helicopter crackled before Blaze answered her rhetorical question, igniting the anger already primed from her frustration, "Depends on the setting, sweetheart."

She ground her teeth together at the endearment delivered in that infuriatingly smug tone of his.

"You want to boss me around in the bedroom? I'm all for it."

Her finger hovered over the emergency release button, and she felt sorely tempted to crush him with the 200 gallons of water she carried in the bucket hanging below the helicopter.

"But you're on my playground now. I'm a hotshot. This is what we do."

The arrogant ass! He'd managed to ask her to bed at least once every day they'd worked together, and she'd rebuffed him each time. For some reason, he kept asking. It grated on her nerves to the point she was ready to kiss him just to shut him up.

What? No, you aren't, Braylin!

Not sure where that thought had come from, she let it feed her fury. She was burning up and not from the lack of air conditioning in the cockpit. The fire licked up her throat as she keyed her mic. "This is my playground too, you—" Braylin cut herself off and took a deep breath. Stooping to his level was exactly what he wanted. She didn't need to give him the satisfaction.

"What was that, angel? You got cut off." Blaze had a smile in his voice like he knew what had stopped her transmission.

A growl left Braylin's lips, and her finger edged closer to the release button. This whole cross-training idea had been ridiculous. The only thing she'd learned from working with Blaze was that he *liked* putting himself in danger. Maybe all hotshots weren't assholes with a hero complex, but she wouldn't bet on it. If he wouldn't heed her warnings, then what was the point of trying to openly communicate between air and ground assets? Of course, she couldn't write that in the report she had to submit to her boss. She'd have to find some way to spin this shitshow into something that didn't stink of her bitterness over the situation.

"Hey, Whitney?"

"What?" she snapped, unable to filter the outrage eating at her chest.

"Do you see what I'm seeing?"

For once, Blaze's voice had lost its seductive edge, so she scanned the spruce and pine trees stretching across the mountainside around his position. Nothing caught her attention among the thick canopy of green. "What are you talking about, Blaze?"

"Smoke."

Is he messing with me?

"I don't see any smoke," she responded as she flew past his location. Or what she *thought* was his location. He'd climbed under the tree line, and his less-than-fresh yellow shirt proved difficult to spot. *Didn't the man know how to do laundry?*

With that thought, she began picturing him naked as he loaded the washer. His sculpted rear end and the muscles in his back bunched as he—Braylin shook her head. What the hell was wrong with her?

"Well, I do, and I'm not talking about the fake kind. We've got a creeper thirty feet north of me."

Braylin blinked the X-rated image away and focused on what he'd said. Her frustration had turned inward, so her voice lost its harshness when she spoke. "All right, fine. Go check it out."

Out of habit, she glanced at her fuel gauge before settling into a holding pattern while Blaze investigated. They were good, but she knew to keep her eye on it because running out of fuel was a death sentence. She might be contemplating getting rid of Blaze, but she didn't want to take herself out in the process.

Her gaze tracked the clouds in the distance, but her thoughts drifted back to his comment about her bossing him around in the bedroom. Though she and B.O.B. had become reacquainted, and she'd spent every night since with her vibrator, it hadn't scratched her itch. If she wanted to stop picturing her and Blaze burning up the sheets, it was time to go on an actual date with someone.

A sigh escaped Braylin's lips at the thought. Finding a date felt like work she wasn't sure she had the energy to put in. But she had to do it if she didn't want to make another colossal mistake. Her past threatened to rear its ugly head, and she shoved it back into the box she kept tightly locked. Besides, she had enough to worry about in the present.

Better to move on.

When she got home, she'd log back into that dating app she used before. Maybe someone would be up for grabbing a drink at the bar tonight. It would at least be a start *and* a step away from the dangerous territory that was Blaze freaking Layne.

"Hey, sweetheart. Miss me?" His bedroom voice sounded in her ears.

Speak of the Devil. She scowled, her eyes narrowing behind her helmet visor. "Would you cut the crap and just tell me what you found?"

"Well, darlin', she's a burning all right. Skunkin' around under the fallen debris."

Her hand tightened on the cyclic, and her voice came out in a near growl. "How is shifting into a southern twang cutting the crap? Can you be serious for once?"

"Angel, you need to loosen up. Humor's a great tool for that. So is sex." He paused for a beat, like he felt she needed to let that sink in. "You should try it sometime."

One. Two. Three. She counted slowly in her head, then took a deep breath and said with deadly certainty, "Blaze, you don't want me to loosen my control. Right now, it's the only thing keeping me from crushing you with two hundred gallons of water. Are we clear?"

She heard the smirk in his tone. "Admit it, sweet thing. You'd miss me if I wasn't around to push your buttons anymore."

She wouldn't dignify that with a response. "Where's the fire?"

At least this time, when he answered, he sounded all business. "I'll walk you in. Look for the panel I laid, start there, and drag the water downhill."

She cracked her neck from side to side, thankful for something else to focus on besides Blaze and the type of release he thought she needed. *Hell, did need.* "Fine. Do you have me in sight?"

His voice warmed, but all he said was, "Yeah, I see you." *Great.* Because she had no clue where *he* was.

"Is the line clear?" She still hadn't spotted his yellow shirt, but he would know to move away from the line where he wanted her to attack the fire.

"Yep. Line's clear." *Good.*

"I've got your panel," she radioed as soon as her eye caught sight of the bright orange plastic. It was a tool wildland firefighters used to mark a line for air assets. Panels were easier to spot than the hotshots' typically dingy yellow shirts. This one looked to be about one foot by four feet long. Braylin turned the aircraft, lining up where Blaze had instructed her to. "Dropping now."

She watched out the side window as the water hit precisely where she'd aimed it. *Bullseye!*

"You soaked me."

With those three words, her high at hitting directly on target dissipated. "Dammit, Blaze! I asked if the line was clear. Why the hell were you standing so close?" If he had another injury, she might just finish him off herself. The absolute last thing she needed was to report this time, it had been *her* fault.

* * *

Standing nearly twenty yards from the panel, Blaze swiped at the droplets dripping down his safety glasses. He'd gotten drenched from the spray after the water hit the ground. Sight clear again, he keyed his transceiver, "We might need to do that again just to work on your aim."

Whitney's scoff came loud and clear through his radio. "My aim is impeccable."

A grin spread across Blaze's face. Riling her up was his new favorite pastime. Maybe because it proved so easy to do. She'd wound herself tighter than a spring, and he wanted to be around when she finally snapped. "Keep telling yourself that, sweetheart."

He knew she hated the nicknames, so he made a point of using them—repeatedly.

He expected her to snap back at him, but the heat had left her voice. When she wasn't using it to berate him, he rather enjoyed the sound of it. She had no discernible accent he could place, but it suited her. A little tough yet still obviously feminine. It made him wonder . . . What had made her so rigid? Every time he'd tried to ask, to make conversation with her this week, she'd shut him down. But he wasn't deterred. Whitney was a challenge, and he *never* threw in the towel.

"Are you injured?" she questioned a second time.

Did she sound genuinely concerned? It surprised him enough that something in Blaze's chest tightened, and he felt the need to reassure her. "No. I wasn't *that* close, angel."

"Good because your head's so big it's hard to miss."

As Blaze chuckled, he thought maybe he did need his head checked since he enjoyed her insults. But she'd just given him the perfect opening. He dropped his voice on the reply. "Why, sweet thing, I'm touched you noticed. I *do* have a big *head*."

After a minute passed without a reply, Blaze worried he might've gone too far with that one. He'd been pretty sure she was attracted to him from the way her stare often lingered a little too long. And what a stare. She had the most intriguing hazel eyes he'd ever seen. They were like mood rings, changing the dominant color from brown to green depending on her emotions. But he still worked on cracking their code.

So far, he'd learned they turned a turbulent sea green whenever she was angry with him. But he'd seen them go a bit hazy, soft brown almost when their eyes stayed locked. So, he'd asked her out. Despite the fact that she kept saying no, he thought she really wanted to say yes. That's why he continued to push. He'd been dropping suggestive comments into their back and forth for days, but . . .

Uncomfortable with the silence, Blaze focused on the smoke he could still see creeping up the hillside. "Whitney? Let's try another drop but a rotor-width to your left this time."

"Now, who's bossy?" He relaxed at the smirk in her tone. If she was back to sparring, he was still in the game. Not wanting to get wet again, he moved further away from the panel as she added,

"This will be it before I need to pick you up and head back."

Watching her steer the helicopter into position, he purred, "You can pick me up anytime, angel."

He admired her skills in handling the machine. The bucket never seemed to swing too wildly, and she knew how to keep the water stream steady when she attacked.

"Keep it up, Blaze. And I'll leave you on the mountain."

He would've responded, but she started to drop. As she flew past, he tucked his head, the sound of the splash drowning out anything he might've said. When the whir of the helicopter rotors grew distant, he hiked back to his panel. She'd thoroughly doused the area, and he didn't see any more smoke. It wasn't a large area of black—where the fire had already burned—but to ensure they'd got it all, he'd have to rake through the debris and extinguish anything still smoldering.

"Looks like we got it, but I'll have to mop up."

"I'm heading for the landing zone. Don't take too long or I *will* leave you. I'm not flying this thing at night." The tinge of fear in her voice convinced him she wasn't kidding. He knew flying in the dark without night vision goggles was risky as hell.

With a groan, Blaze wiped the sweat off his forehead. Mopping up in the black went hella faster with a crew of twenty, and he didn't particularly want to spend the night out here. *Especially* when he had other plans for how they could spend it. Grinning at the thought, Blaze pulled out his McLeod and got to work.

CHAPTER 5

You Think You Know a Person

Braylin leaned both hands on either side of the white utility sink in the bathroom of Backyard Barb's and stared at her reflection in the double mirror above it. Trimmed in chrome like the sink, it harkened back to a previous decade. The whole bar had the same throwback vibe, not that she cared much about the décor. But focusing on the red subway tiles lining the wall behind the sink or even the floor's covering of stickers from various places and events—some scuffed to the point of being unrecognizable—was better than thinking about what had happened an hour ago.

In the mirror, her reflection cringed, and Braylin let out a heavy sigh before turning on the faucet to scrub down her arms. They were bare in the black lace tank top she'd donned for her date. She didn't consider herself a germaphobe, but the plush, cushioned rim lining the bar she'd been sitting at moments ago gave her the urge to sanitize, sanitize. Despite trying not to touch the barrier, her arms had brushed it a few times. She'd been struggling not to think about how much bacteria lived in that thing after decades of people leaning against it, spilling drinks on it, and who knew what else.

Braylin cut off the water and reached for the brown paper towels on a rack to her left. She was on a date. She *should* be enjoying herself, but she couldn't when her thoughts kept straying to the incident with her crew chief.

At the lack of truth in her statement, a snort of derision twisted the features she'd bothered to highlight with makeup. Putting in that much effort was a rare occasion for Braylin, but she'd actually been excited when the Clark Kent look-alike agreed to go out with her tonight. Her date—Steve—seemed nice enough, but from what she could tell, they had *nothing* in common.

For the last half hour, Braylin had been struggling to find something to talk about, and she didn't know how much more she could take. He was a nature photographer, and though she enjoyed a beautiful picture as much as the next person, she couldn't stand to listen to another lecture on how to capture the exact lighting you wanted.

After the day she'd had, she was afraid she'd be bored to *literal* tears. Within the first five minutes, it had become painfully obvious that Steve wouldn't scratch her itch, and she needed a polite way to cut this date short. She'd escaped to the bathroom for a breather, but now she wondered how long she'd have to stay there for him to just leave.

Like, I'd be that lucky.

A scowl narrowed her eyes and turned down her painted lips. She crumpled the used paper, then tossed it into a bin by the door. Her luck was on a downward spiral. Evidenced by the fact Blaze's charm started to get to her. Maybe it had been spurred on by the relief that she hadn't accidentally crushed him with her drop, but she'd enjoyed bickering with him on the flight home this afternoon. Enough so that her guard had slipped, and she'd smiled at him. As soon as she'd realized what she'd been doing, she'd cut that out, reminding herself she didn't date guys she worked with, not after what Rob had done to her.

Not tonight. She couldn't relive the disaster of

her relationship with her ex tonight. Not when she was already raw from everything else that had been dumped on her head. As if she didn't have enough to worry about dealing with Blaze daily, now she had the problem with Roger. She and her crew chief had disagreements before, but the fight they'd gotten into an hour ago had been something else. It still burned like jet fuel in her gut.

Reliving it, Braylin's hand went to her stomach as if she could soothe the sting. On the way back to the hangar this afternoon, she noticed an issue with the fuel gauge. She'd been tracking it carefully, so when it had a reading she knew couldn't be accurate, she'd meant to tell her crew chief about it when they landed. But then Blaze had asked her out—again. She'd let him rile her up so much that desperation to get him off her back shifted all her focus to finding a date, and the fuel issue had slipped her mind.

They were working out of the town where Leif Aero's hangar sat, and she lived close enough to sleep in her own bed every night. She didn't know or care where Blaze had chosen to stay. She'd been trying her damnedest to keep thoughts of Blaze and his bed from entering her mind. She didn't want to think about where it was or who filled it.

A bud of jealousy unfurled in her chest, and Braylin snapped it off, forcing away the image of Blaze with another woman.

Get a grip, Whitney.

She'd been in the middle of adding waves to her hair in preparation for her date with Steve when she remembered the problem with the fuel gauge. Since her apartment was only fifteen minutes from the hangar, she hadn't minded stopping by on her way to the bar to let Roger know about it. He was scheduled for the night shift tonight, and she figured she'd be able to catch him so the crew could check the fuel system out before they were off tomorrow.

It had been clear he wasn't expecting to see her when she'd barged into his office.

Like a kid caught stealing a cookie before dinner, Roger had dropped the phone he'd been using to take photos, jumping to his feet with wide eyes. "Whitney! What are you doing here?"

At first, Braylin had been confused until she recognized the equipment sitting on his desk. Her stomach had twisted into knots before she'd met his gaze. "Isn't that the part we're out of?"

He'd told her that morning the GPS had failed update, and they'd have to order a new one in. It was an expensive piece of avionics, but not something she *had* to have to fly the aircraft. Because it wasn't on the minimum equipment list for flight, she'd merely shrugged and not minded waiting the three days he'd said it would take to get one in. But to find he'd already had it . . . she'd watched Roger regain his composure and scrambled her brain for a reason why he would've lied to her.

"Yeah."

When he hadn't elaborated, she'd pushed. "Did it come in that quickly or . . ." She'd crossed her arms over her chest and stared him down.

He'd audibly swallowed, then scrubbed at his neck. "Look, Whit. I don't want to lie to you, but . . ."

Those knots in her stomach had tightened. "But what, Roger?"

He'd sunk into his chair and dropped his head in his hands. "I'm in trouble." When he'd lifted his gaze to hers, his dark brown eyes had pleaded. "I need the money, or some very bad people are coming after me."

Braylin blinked and shook the memory away. She knew what she had to do about Roger; she just didn't want to do it. Didn't want to believe it, honestly. He'd been her ally, her friend, and now . . . she couldn't trust him or his judgment. Not if he was addicted to gambling and had resorted to selling the company's parts for cash.

You think you know a person. She winced against the slice of pain that followed.

Before she could recover, the bathroom door swung open, nearly catching her where she'd stood in front of it, and the noise of the latest country song playing louder than anyone not half deaf or drunk could endure blasted into her space. Braylin backed up a step as a curvy middle-aged blonde blustered in, singing along to the tune.

The woman stopped mid-note when she caught sight of Braylin. "Oh, sugar." Her deep blue eyes softened as they took in Braylin's expression. "Do you need me to throw someone out?"

"What?" Braylin's forehead pinched in confusion.

"You've got that look." Her red-painted nails flashed as she placed her hands on her ample jean-clad hips. "Is someone botherin' you?" She shook her mass of blonde curls. "No need to hide out in here. You just show me which one, and he's gone."

Braylin didn't know who this woman was, but she appreciated the sentiment. A wan smile graced her lips in response. "No, just a tough day."

The woman stared her down like she didn't believe her. "If you're sure . . ."

When she trailed off, Braylin asked, "I'm sorry, but *who* are you?"

"Oh," she chuckled and held out a hand before continuing, "I'm Barbara, though everyone calls me Barb. This is my place, so the offer still stands." She winked and smiled.

The woman's energy proved infectious, and Braylin found herself smiling back as she shook her hand. "Thanks, Barb, but it's not that kind of problem."

"Well, if whiskey's not solving your troubles, maybe you need a different kind of stiff one." She half-bent over, slapping her thigh with a cackle, then added, "If you catch my drift."

Heat flooded Braylin's face. Not at the woman's brashness but because she'd echoed Blaze's remark, making her the second person to tell Braylin that in the last 24 hours.

Is it that obvious?

"Oh, shoot. I've embarrassed you. Don't mind my mouth. It gets me in trouble at the best of times." Barb didn't wait for her response; she just patted Braylin's arm and entered one of the stalls.

Blowing out a breath, Braylin faced the mirror again. She almost laughed at the resting bitch face she wore. It might work to get rid of Steve, but the poor guy didn't deserve that. Forcing a smile to her lips, she smoothed her hair and pushed thoughts of anything but her date out of her mind. When her teeth wanted to grit, she forced them to relax and reached for the bathroom door.

* * *

Blaze whistled as he pushed open the door to Backyard Barb's, the only decent watering hole in town, his mood chipper despite being turned down by Whitney—again. He'd started to chip away at her armor, no matter how slowly.

On the way back to the hangar that afternoon, she'd actually smiled at him until she'd realized what she was doing and quickly squashed it. But he'd seen it, and it had been a beautiful sight. The green in her eyes glinted when she smiled. He looked forward to Monday and the chance to pull another one from her.

Maybe he'd get lucky and even run into her this weekend. They were working out of Granby, Colorado, and the town was small. With barely over two thousand residents, he figured his odds were pretty good. He'd been to Granby before while working on a fire. It nestled at the base of Mount Chauncey and had some great hiking trails, but his accommodations at the Trail Blazer Motel weren't much of a step above fire camp. The one thing it had going for it was being within walking distance of a handful of restaurants and his second favorite woman in town—Barb. If he couldn't spend his Friday night with Whitney, he'd hang out with the animated blonde.

He'd met Barb two years ago, but as soon as he walked back into her bar, she recognized him and gave him drinks on the house. She was like the fun aunt who gave you condoms or bought you beer before you were old enough.

Blaze stepped inside to the sound of country music playing loudly over the bar's speakers. Like Barb herself, everything about the place was loud. The music, the bright red booths lining the far wall, even the reflective chrome that covered an oval, dropped ceiling above the dark wood bar centered in the middle of the room. It felt like a diner and a dive bar had a baby. The décor shouldn't work, but somehow, the woman herself tied it all together.

Catching sight of her blonde curls, Blaze smiled and followed Barb to the opposite side of the bar top. He'd made it halfway when the sight in front of him froze his feet to the sticky linoleum floor.

He knew Whitney was hot, but the way she looked tonight? *Fucking gorgeous.* Her hair fell around her shoulders and halfway down her back in smooth chocolate waves. Her lids were outlined, and her lashes highlighted, making those hazel eyes a deep smoky color. And her lips . . . his stomach muscles tightened in anticipation at the thought of those bright red lips wrapped around his di—

"Blaze!"

At the shriek of his name, his head whipped away from Whitney to see Barb waving at him from behind the bar. He responded with a nod but glanced back at Whitney.

Her smoky eyes had narrowed, and her red-hot mouth pursed in a thin line as she stared at him. The obvious annoyance in her expression delighted him to no end.

The odds are *in my favor.*

Blaze gave her a wide grin before going to greet the blonde. Copping a squat on a stool with a direct view of Whitney, he asked Barb, "How's my favorite lady tonight?"

"Oh, you sweet talker," she drawled. "I bet you call everyone your favorite."

"Nah, only the pretty ones." He winked, and she dropped her head back on a cackle.

While she laughed, Blaze glanced over at Whitney, just now noticing the man she sat with.

Who is this hipster?

A frown crept over Blaze's expression. Is that who Whitney was into? Clean-shaven, artsy types in horn-rimmed glasses and ironic t-shirts?

Barb slapped his arm playfully, dragging his attention away. "I knew I liked you. What're you drinking this evening, handsome?"

"I'll have a Coors."

"Draft?"

He'd already turned away to watch Whitney again, so his response was a "Huh?"

Barb raised an eyebrow.

Blaze blinked. What had she asked him?

"On draft or bottle?"

Oh. "Draft is good."

Instead of turning away to pull his beer, Barb smirked at him. With a nod in Whitney's direction, she said, "She's a pretty one, that's for sure. I'd say you could save her from that poor sucker she's been stuck next to for the last half hour, but I think she'd shoot you down as soon as thank you."

Now, Blaze smirked. "I like a challenge. In fact"—the creases in his cheeks deepened with a mischievous grin—"why don't you refill their drinks with my compliments."

Barb chuckled as she walked away to fill the drink order, and he turned his attention back to Whitney. She smiled at something Glasses said, but it didn't reach her eyes. There was no glow in them like he'd seen that afternoon. The realization sent a punch of satisfaction through him. Maybe hipster wasn't her type after all. She caught him staring and scowled.

Blaze turned away with a smile right as Barb set his pint of Coors on the scarred wood of the bar top. He leaned in, resting his elbows on the black cushion that rimmed it, and took a long sip. "Thanks, beautiful." He grabbed Barb's hand and kissed the back of it, making her squeal with glee. "You pull the best pint of Coors in Colorado."

She freed her fingers, swatting at his arm. "You're so full of it." Her blue eyes twinkled as she glanced toward Whitney. "Now, let's see what she makes of your gesture."

Barb leaned against the wood, and they both watched as a lanky young bartender delivered the drinks Blaze had ordered. Whitney opened her mouth to protest—he felt sure—but the bartender waved in his direction, and her bright lips slammed shut. The glare she aimed his way could've cut glass; it was so sharp.

Barb straightened next to him, laughing. "Looks like you struck out, Blaze. Better luck next game."

He grinned in reply, eyes and ears strained in Whitney's direction. "Game's not over yet."

Blaze finished his first beer and then started on another while trying to watch Whitney and Glasses without getting caught. She didn't touch the drink he'd sent over, but her companion downed his.

Fifteen minutes later, Glasses was getting handsy. Blaze frowned at the palm he'd placed on Whitney's bare shoulder. She shrugged it off, but the guy didn't take the hint, turning more into her and putting a hand on her jean-clad thigh. Again, she shrugged him off, but the guy was dense or had too much to drink because he didn't get the memo that she wasn't interested. Blaze could tell from ten feet away.

Idiot.

He watched closely, curious how exactly Whitney would lay into the guy. Blaze had been on the receiving end of her anger often enough to know it had a short fuse. She scooted further away from Glasses to the point her ass had to be half hanging off the stool, but that was it. No sharp retort, no cutting words to make it clear exactly where they stood.

Wait, is she only that mean to me?

Glasses' hand returned to her shoulder, and he leaned in like he would kiss her. Whitney popped off her stool. The tortured expression on her face dragged Blaze to his feet, and he stood behind her in two quick strides.

"Hey, Whit. Need some help?"

Hipster dude blinked up at him, then tried to reach for Whitney again, but she backed up a step—into Blaze. She stomped on his foot, probably on purpose, before moving to stand by his side.

Glasses glanced confusedly between him and Whitney. "What's going on? I thought your name was Braylin?"

The fuck?

Blaze's eyes widened as he stared down at her. The color of hers shifted to the turbulent sea green, which meant she was livid. But she wasn't the only one angry at the moment. Had she given him a false name or . . . *shit.* "Your name's Braylin?" His voice sounded surprisingly calm compared to the rapid beat of his pulse.

He didn't think she could glare any harder, but somehow, he felt it, the fury burning up and out through her eyes. "Yes," she hissed, "Braylin

Whitney."

The admission cut him like a knife, and he sucked in a sharp breath. "Geez, Whit"—he stopped, shaking his head—"I mean Braylin. We've been working together for days, and you didn't want to tell me that? Why?"

Why did not knowing her name hurt so damned much? It felt like a knife had punctured his lung, and breathing became difficult. Then, his thoughts scattered on a barrage of questions.

Why didn't she want him to know?

She'd basically lied to him the whole time they'd known each other.

Or was it a manipulation tactic? Was he somehow at fault for not asking in the first place?

Damn, maybe she's more like Sloane than I thought.

"Excuse me," Glasses started, and Braylin cut in.

"Steve, it's been fun, but I need to call it a night." She reached for her purse hanging on the hook under the bar top while Blaze stood stunned, his world in turmoil.

"Oh, but—" Glasses' hand landed on Braylin's arm again, and Blaze's cool edged dangerously close to slipping away.

He cut Steve off, "She's not interested, dude.

Move on." Disconnecting them, he grabbed Braylin's hand.

She said nothing as he dragged her toward the hall that branched into the kitchen and bathrooms. In front of a door marked 'storage' he paused and turned, looking to make sure Steve had left.

When he didn't see any sign of the guy, he pushed away the disappointment eating at his gut and asked her again. "Why didn't you tell me?"

CHAPTER 6

What's in a Name?

Why hadn't she?

Braylin stared up at Blaze's face. For once, his cocky smirk was nowhere to be found. Even his eyes had lost their gleam. She pursed her lips.

Is he upset with me? *Seriously?*

The anger still on simmer from her fight with Roger had been stoked into a low burn after seeing Blaze walk into the bar. She'd even endured another round with Steve just to avoid him. Then he'd come butting into her business anyway.

Cocky jerk.

Now, her gaze heated as she thought about his question. After she'd rescued him from the wildfire, Braylin hadn't bothered to tell Blaze her full name because she'd never expected to see him again. But then she'd gotten stuck working with him.

"Why didn't you ask?" she threw back, crossing her arms over her chest and raising an eyebrow. A lot of pilots wore name tags with only their surnames or even a call sign embroidered on them. Maybe it was petty, but she'd wanted him to ask, and when he hadn't, she'd let it go, figuring if he didn't care enough to find out her first name, then why bother telling him? She'd hoped to be free of him as soon as possible, and the less he knew about her, the better.

He mirrored her pose. "So it's my fault?"

Usually, the challenge in his response would've had her snapping at him, but the day's events caught up with her, dousing her usual fire like an ice bath. She'd fought enough for one day. Dropping her arms with a sigh, Braylin told him, "Whatever."

She turned on her heel, ready to go home and wallow, but Blaze stopped her. Before she realized what was happening, his hand moved in her hair, sliding up to cup her head and turning her to face him.

"Angel," his baritone voice softened as he tilted her face so that she was forced to look into his eyes. The blue had deepened to the color of a pool at night, tempting her to drown her sorrows in it. "What's wrong?"

Braylin shut her lids against the concern she glimpsed on his face. "Please don't be nice to me," she whisper-groaned.

She couldn't handle him being nice. Not when her control hung on by a thread. It was so much worse—resisting him—when he stood this close. She could smell his cologne, and the birchwood scent made her want to lean in and get a deeper whiff. A thin layer of smoke underlay it, but it was pleasant, like cooking s'mores over a campfire.

Is it part of his cologne, or does the scent linger because of his job?

Blaze's thumbs brushed her temples as he said, "Tell me, Braylin."

No. She didn't want to talk—or even think— about her fight with Roger anymore *or* her dud of a date with Steve. What she wanted . . . what she wanted was Blaze.

Braylin's eyes popped open, and before she could talk herself out of it, she stood on her toes and crushed her mouth to his. Blaze's lips were soft but stiff. She felt his surprise in that first frozen moment, but it quickly morphed into hunger.

His hands slid down to her waist and pulled her against him. The press of their bodies together stoked the attraction she could no longer ignore. Her hands lifted to hold his head, tangling in his blonde waves. She wasn't sure who opened first, but the kiss heated, turning into a duel of tongues. Even in this, they fought, but it was a battle Braylin relished entering—win or lose.

The stubble on Blaze's skin scratched her face and sent a thrill arrowing to her core. She let it warm her up as she pushed her aching breasts into the hard muscles of his chest and tasted him. The slightly sweet, malty flavor of the beer he'd drunk coated her tongue, but underneath it she tasted a subtle smokiness she craved. Rubbing her heat against the growing bulge in his pants, a moan shook her throat as the wildfire she'd been trying to put out since they'd first met, jumped the line.

God, she needed this.

But it wasn't enough. She wanted more. Now.

Breaking the kiss, she glanced around the hallway. They were alone, but anyone could come back here. Her eyes fell on the door labeled 'storage' right as Blaze uttered, "Whoa."

She would've smirked in satisfaction when she caught his dazed expression, but she'd become a woman on a mission. Grabbing his arm, she used the other hand to reach for the doorknob.

Please be unlocked.

It was. Braylin's grin looked a little unhinged as she opened the storage room and dragged Blaze inside. Her hand slapped the wall, searching for a light switch.

Bingo.

A dim overhead bulb illuminated a narrow stack of shelving filled with paper products and cleaning supplies lining the side and back walls in an "L" that wrapped around the room. Satisfied it would work for her purposes, Braylin shut the door behind them, locked it, and pushed Blaze up against it.

His sky-colored eyes widened as his back hit the wood. "What are you doing?"

"Isn't it obvious?" Braylin stripped off her tank top and reached for his hand to place it on her chest.

This time, he didn't hesitate. His lids half closed as he pushed off the door to get a better hold of her. Her head fell back as his large palms massaged her bare breasts. When his head lowered, the whisper of his breath sent a quiver of need coursing through her, pebbling her exposed skin.

"Is this real?"

Instead of answering, she began unbuttoning her jeans. His tongue trailed down her neck, slowing her progress as a shiver racked her body. When his mouth closed over her sensitive peak, a warmth as deep and dark as the rum she had drunk followed it, threatening to send her into dangerous territory—where this became more than just sex.

No. A thread of panic tugged at Braylin's belly, and she allowed it to pull her away from the possibility of what they were doing turning into something more.

Sex. A release. That's all this is.

Repeating it like a mantra, she guided Blaze's hand where she needed it. When his palm cupped her mound, she closed her eyes on a punch of pleasure. "Do you have a condom?"

"Fuck, you're wet," he said with a choked breath.

She knew it, could feel it soaking her underwear. That's why she was ready to do something about it. When his fingers grazed her most sensitive spot, she hissed through her teeth, "Condom?"

"No." Blaze didn't lift his gaze as his fingers dipped under the elastic. He teased her, saying,

"Contrary to popular belief, I didn't come here tonight to get lucky."

His fingers made it hard to concentrate. The walls buzzed with the muffled beat of the country music from the bar, and it felt like the same thrum vibrated at the apex of her thighs. Braylin's legs wanted to shake, to give in to what Blaze made her feel, but this was important, so she forced herself to hold on and focus. On a gasp of breath, she managed, "I have an implant. Are you clean?"

"Yeah, but"—Blaze removed his hand from between her legs, and she watched him struggle to find a measure of control as his gaze raked up her body to her face—"are you sure about this?"

A laugh—half anger, half disbelief—bubbled out of her. "Are you kidding me right now? You've been trying to get into my pants since the day we met."

He said nothing to that, and she knew she had him there. To prove it, she pushed her jeans the rest of the way down her legs, taking her underwear with them. She was too far gone to care about the state of the floor on her bare feet as she slung off the flats she wore. Her pants followed until she stood naked in front of a fully clothed Blaze.

"Angel—"

She cut off any other objection, reaching for his belt buckle. "Blaze, less talking. More fucking."

Eyeing her, he pulled his shirt off and tossed it to the floor. "You're so damn bossy."

"Why are you still talking?" She got a glimpse of defined abdominal muscles before she started to push his pants down.

Blaze stilled her busy hands. "Come here." He tilted her face up, and then his lips covered hers. The kiss was as hot as the one they'd shared before, but this time, the heat wasn't the fast-burning flames of a brush fire. It proved way more deadly, starting in her chest and building outward, slowly filling her veins with a languid warmth that had the power to lull her into submission.

Braylin leaned into him, drinking in the dizzying flavor of his lips. Sweet and smoky, she let him fill her tastebuds, her senses.

Have I ever been kissed like this before?

His hands caressed her cheek, her neck, flooding her body with sensation everywhere those calloused fingers touched. Blaze kissed her as if he could do only that for hours and be satisfied. Braylin found herself willing to let him try.

Danger, Will Robinson!

A warning bell rang in her head, and she forced their mouths apart.

You don't like him. This is just sex.

Even though she told herself those words, Braylin wasn't sure she believed them. "Pants off." At least her voice came out strong and in control despite the knots her insides were tangling into.

"Are you sure you can handle this?" His eyes taunted her as he waved a hand over himself.

His teasing would've made her smile, but she'd put a lid on her emotions, then locked it for good measure. She would *not* let herself fall for him. Her hands landed on her hips. "Off, Blaze."

He kicked off his boots, then held her gaze as he hooked a thumb on either side of his boxer briefs. Torturously slow, he lowered them with his pants.

Braylin couldn't pull her eyes away, the slow-motion strip tease arousing her more than it should've. Her gaze traced the line above his hip as it funneled inward, devouring every tan, sculpted inch of him. When his length sprang free, she might've salivated a little.

At least he hadn't lied about having a big head.

Her inner voice snickered, then took in the

dark blonde hair covering his muscular thighs and calves. After Blaze's pants cleared his ankles, he tossed them to join the pile of clothing they'd made, and Braylin pounced. Though a part of her wanted to touch him, to return the teasing his fingers had given her, she told herself this was about *her* pleasure, not his.

Hooking her arms around his neck, she demanded, "Lift me."

A spark flared in his eyes before his hands cupped her ass. He bent his head, his body curving around hers, causing her nerve endings to fire in a delirious frenzy as he said low in her ear, "Jump."

She did, and he caught her, wrapping her legs around his waist. His erection rubbed against her slit, and she bit back a moan. She'd wanted fast, but this wasn't fast enough. Braylin tensed, ready to lift up and drive Blaze home when he turned them around. Her back connected with the cold of the door, and she hissed out a breath. Then Blaze's mouth claimed hers, swallowing the angry retort she'd intended to throw at him.

As the kiss heated, so did her blood. The need to have Blaze inside her morphed into an ache that throbbed with every beat of her pulse. Desperate to answer her body's demand, Braylin's fingers reached to guide him in.

When her hand closed around his shaft, Blaze groaned, breaking their kiss. "Angel—"

"Now." Braylin didn't wait for whatever he wanted to say, not when there was a chance he'd try to slow them down. Lifting her hips, she took him in. It'd been too long since she'd felt that stretch. She pushed him to the hilt, biting her lip as pleasure roared through her.

Finally.

"Fuuuck," Blaze muttered as one hand slapped the door above her head. He'd closed his eyes, and his jaw clenched so tight she could see the muscle bulging under his golden scruff. His other hand gripped her ass cheek hard enough to leave a bruise. She didn't care.

"That's right, Blaze. Fuck me." Braylin panted, shifting her hips to rock into him, and felt his whole body tremble in response.

When he looked at her, the black of his pupils eclipsed the blue in his eyes. Something wild stirred in their depths as he said, "Hold onto me."

Braylin hooked her arms around each of Blaze's and clenched her legs on his hips as he drove into her. The noise of them slamming into the door echoed in her ears, but somehow, it sounded distant. She didn't care that people could hear them. Right now, in this moment, nothing else existed. Just her and him and the slide of their bodies together.

The rhythm they set was fast and feverish, a race against a blaze they couldn't contain. As the heat grew, the fact that this was a bad idea kept screaming in Braylin's head, but she silenced it. After the day she'd had, she just wanted to feel good, no matter how fleeting it might be.

Surrendering to the fire building in her blood, she let the flames of her need burn the doubts away until she became merely a woman attracted to a man, giving and taking pleasure where she pleased. There was no Braylin and no Blaze.

Each thrust drove her closer until the inferno they'd created together burst into a wildfire of epic proportions. Braylin's cry muffled against Blaze's shoulder as she bit down, triggering his release, and they collapsed against the door. The arm holding her up shook. It was the only thing supporting her weight because her legs had gone slack when she'd come.

Too quickly, the blissful feeling from her orgasm dissipated, and she tried to lower herself. The fire that had burned through her turned to ash in her veins.

What have I done?

"You can put me down now." Her voice was almost a croak as panic constricted her airways, and Braylin had to swallow to wet her dry throat. "Blaze?"

He hadn't moved or acknowledged her statement. His head leaned against the wall next to hers, and she ran a hand through his hair before she had time to talk herself out of it. He grunted something unintelligible, making her frown.

Braylin tried to wriggle out of his grasp with a desperate, "Put me down."

As sharply as she'd needed that release, she now needed to flee. Regrets flooded in, washing over her like a physical wave. "Put me down," she said again, this time, her tone harsh.

Blaze's arm slid from underneath her as he slowly leaned back, shaking his head. "That was . . ."

"Save it. I know exactly what that was," Braylin snapped, grabbing at clothing and hoping it belonged to her. She had to get dressed so she could get the hell out of this closet.

"We're back to fighting?" She did *not* hear disappointment in his question. *Did not.*

Braylin shoved her legs in her jeans. "Yep, this changes nothing." To drive that point home, she speared him with her stare. "And it's never going to happen again."

The cocky bastard smirked at her. "Whatever you say, sweet thing."

A frustrated growl left her throat as she slammed her tank top on. But her bitchiness was a cover, one she was losing a grip on. She felt it—the prick of tears—and knew she had to escape before they fell.

Braylin reached for the door. Opening it, she tossed him a smirk of her own. "Thanks for the ride, hotshot."

* * *

Braylin stood under the near-scalding spray of the shower and pressed her heated forehead against the cold white tiles. A tear tracked down her right cheek, and she flung it away with an angry swipe. She hated crying. It made her feel weak—something she preferred to avoid. But despite her best efforts, the salty traitors still fell.

Because she had sex with Blaze. It was the cherry on top of her night from Hell.

Braylin scowled and wished the hot water could wash away the memory of her complete and total fuckup as easily as it had gotten rid of the evidence of their joining.

What had she been thinking?

Oh wait, you weren't.

The thought made her cringe, and a horrible sound—half sob, half deprecating laugh—tore at her throat. She'd made her rule about not getting involved with guys she worked with for a reason.

Or have you forgotten?

As if she needed the reminder, Braylin's mind conjured up the events of her past. Like a sadistic trip down memory lane, every toxic instance with her ex-boyfriend assaulted her senses. Though she clenched her lids shut, she could see, hear, and smell him. A shudder wracked her frame.

He'd been tall and cocky too. But also fair and smoothly good-looking with his boy-next-door face and shock of umber hair that always managed to carry the scents of apricot and engine exhaust. Unable to stop the scenes with Rob from flashing in her head, Braylin slid to the floor of the shower, sobs shaking her body as she hugged her arms around her legs and lowered her head to her knees.

His whittling her down to nothing had been a slow process. So slow she hadn't noticed what was happening until it had been too late. The relationship had ended over three years ago, but shame flooded Braylin over the fact that it had taken her more than a year to notice what he'd been doing to her. Remembering, she dug her fingernails into the soft flesh of her upper arms. The physical pain might've been punishment; a part of her still blamed herself for falling under Rob's spell.

She'd been so stupidly in love. So blind.

They'd been part of the same aviation battalion in the Army. Rob had been a helicopter pilot, too, and she'd loved how much they had in common. How comfortable it had been to be with someone who understood the military lingo and faced the same work struggles. But that love had turned sour when she'd finally opened her eyes.

He'd never physically abused her. That she could've *seen*, could've defended against.

To Braylin, what Rob did was worse. He'd made her feel small, insignificant, unworthy even. Tearing her down until her performance at her job had suffered—just like he'd wanted. She'd gone from being on top, the first officer up for praise and advancement, to being sneered at by her peers. The humiliation still echoed hollowly in her chest.

She'd let him ruin her.

Useless tears escaped with a howl as she beat her fists against the shower floor.

Rob's attack had occurred on two fronts. He'd twisted words and events in that ever-reasonable voice of his, always making her see his side and sympathize with him . . . until she'd lost herself in the process.

At the same time he'd been manipulating her, he'd been devaluating her position behind her back. Spreading rumors and lies among the other officers. He'd called her integrity into question and sown seeds of doubt in their minds, telling them she wouldn't hesitate to throw any of them under the bus if it meant she'd get ahead.

Ruthless. Conniving. Fake. That's how Rob had painted her.

When she'd finally realized what he had done, she'd confronted him, then pleaded her case with her brothers and sisters—her fellow Mustangs—who should've had her back. But Rob's campaign had been too thorough, and he'd beaten her. She'd seen the defeat in her friend's gazes as they refused to believe her accusations about him. Being a pawn he'd moved strategically out of his way, had left her broken.

So she'd left. Finished out her time with the 2nd General Support Aviation Battalion and said goodbye to Uncle Sam, vowing never to get wrapped up in a guy she worked with *ever* again.

Flying with Leif Aero had been a chance to start over in a new industry with new people, and now she'd jeopardized that by sleeping with Blaze.

Fresh anger at herself over breaking her vow clenched Braylin's teeth as she pushed to her feet. The water turned cold, but she didn't move from under the spray. She deserved to suffer because now she was set to repeat her wretched history.

Maybe the problem was . . . *her*. Maybe she was a magnet for bad relationships. Blaze might not be gunning for her job, but he could easily ruin her reputation within the industry. It was hard enough just being a woman in a male-dominated field. Any little indiscretion and her competency could be called into question.

Fuck!

Emotionally exhausted, she slapped off the water. Shivering from the chill droplets left on her skin, she stepped out of the shower and toweled off before climbing under the covers of her king-sized bed. Tonight, the expanse of it made her feel especially empty. Her eyes pricked, but she had no tears left.

Braylin hugged the navy coverlet to her chest as her teeth threatened to chatter. Closing her eyes, she forced herself to face the issue with Blaze. She couldn't go back in time, so her options were limited. Either pretend what they'd shared never happened ... A cramp pinched her stomach and spread.

Or she could be a grown-up and ask him to keep what happened separate from their professional relationship.

Internally, she sighed. That meant Blaze had to act like an adult, too, and she wasn't sure he was capable of being serious about anything.

Heaven help me.

CHAPTER 7

Shit, Meet Fan

Monday morning hadn't come fast enough for Blaze. The weekend had dragged on as he'd waited to see Braylin again. Especially after he'd thought he'd seen tears shining in her eyes Friday night. But then, they'd been clear when she'd turned with that parting shot thanking him for the ride. Clear and back to cool, the dominant color a frosty pale green.

The woman confused the hell out of him. He wasn't sure if he should be pissed at her for using him or thankful she had.

Maybe both.

Debating it, Blaze frowned out the windshield of his battered black truck while he drove to the hangar. He *should* be happy.

You got what you wanted.

Despite what he told himself, it felt hollow, the words as empty as the pit in his stomach. He couldn't deny the sex had been phenomenal—the kind he would spend years fantasizing over—but *damn*, he wanted more.

A repeat at the earliest opportunity, only they'd take it slow this time.

He'd set a leisurely pace, exploring every inch of that lithe body until she finally let go of the control she had a death grip on.

What would Braylin be like if she loosened up? Gave into him?

Imagining it, Blaze nearly ran off the road. When a car blared its horn, he blinked and corrected into his lane. He had it bad. And unless he wanted to show up to work with a hard-on, he needed to think about something else.

Should he have followed her that night? She'd clearly been upset about something, and instead of talking about it, he'd ended up fucking her against the wall. And while he in no way regretted that, Blaze had hoped it would change Braylin's attitude toward him, but she'd made it clear that wasn't going to happen.

Flashes of Friday night bombarded him. He could admit he should've asked her full name instead of assuming Whitney was the proper one. Braylin didn't seem to be holding that against him, at least not more than anything else he'd done to piss her off.

His hands tightened around the wheel as the pit in his stomach stretched wider. He'd let go of that initial hurt he'd felt over not knowing her name, but her telling him what they'd shared meant nothing; it had been a fresh puncture to his lungs. Remembering it, he felt a pinch in his chest, and Blaze coughed out a breath.

I'll change her mind.

Meeting her on the job should work in his favor. She was in her element at Leif Aero, and he admired the rapport she seemed to have with her maintenance crew. They often made jokes and ragged on each other, which never failed to make her smile. He'd wished she would turn those smiles on him, but the first and only one she'd given him had ended too abruptly.

Here's hoping.

When Blaze walked into the hangar fifteen minutes later, the bitter atmosphere took him by surprise. No smiles. No jokes this morning. Just complete and frosty silence. As one of the maintenance crew worked on a helicopter part, the clanging of a wrench echoed across the cement floor with no other noise to drown it out.

Squinting against the rising sun coming in the open bay door, Blaze searched for Braylin. When he didn't see her, he headed for the office to his right, passing a couple of maintainers whose scowls made him wonder what had gone down. He was about to ask who pissed in their cereal when shouting drew his attention away.

Braylin's voice rang out over the heated timbre of a male tone, carrying through the open office door. Blaze frowned at the anger apparent in both.

Hoping to dispel their argument, he picked up his pace and entered the hangar's small outer office.

Before he had time to intervene, Braylin flew out of the doorway on his left. She growled at him—*not a great sign*—then pushed past without even a word. He frowned after her as she stomped toward the helicopter.

Blaze scratched at the scruff on his chin and sighed. Today was off to a rippin' start.

"I'd let her cool down a few minutes before you head over there." The male voice he'd heard said from behind.

Blaze turned to find a balding middle-aged man he hadn't met yet, shaking his head. "What happened?"

The man grumbled, then lowered his voice. "I'm taking over for Roger as crew chief, and she's not happy about it."

"How come?"

The man just shrugged and didn't meet his gaze. Blaze could tell there was more to the story, but he'd rather hear it from Braylin.

He started in her direction, and the man called out, "Good luck!"

Blaze just waved him off. A livid Braylin didn't scare him. He'd become well-acquainted with that side of her personality.

As he neared the helicopter, he heard angry muttering. Following the sound, he found Braylin bent over, looking at some panel inside the chopper. The view was outstanding—her tight ass raised in the air gave him all kinds of ideas—and he took a minute to admire the perfect shape of it.

She must've sensed him staring because she spun around, raising the tiny flashlight in her hand like a weapon. "Motherfu—"

"Morning, Braylin." He cut off her curse with a grin.

"Blaze," she gritted out through clenched teeth but lowered the weapon.

"Do you need any help?"

"Not from you." She tapped the flashlight in the palm of her hand, mumbling something that sounded a lot like, "You've done enough."

Ouch.

Not the best opening, but he didn't give up. Ever.

As she glared at him, he debated his next move. He could give her some space, *or* he could add fuel to the fire burning in those lovely hazel eyes until it gained enough momentum to break free. That option seemed more appealing, so Blaze shrugged deliberately, then climbed into the co-pilot seat, pushing it back as far as it would go before crossing his arms behind his head and closing his lids.

"Just tell me when we're ready to take off then, sweet thing."

* * *

Braylin's chest heaved with every fuming breath as she stared at Blaze's relaxed posture. Her hand clenched around the flashlight, and she thought longer than she should've about throwing it at his head.

If last Friday had been bad, this morning was set to top it. She shouldn't be surprised how fast the front office replaced Roger once she'd reported him, but she'd hoped for the chance to talk to the rest of the crew before that happened. Instead, she'd shown up early this morning, and the rumor mill had gotten to them first. Now everyone was pissed at her. *She* was the bad guy. No matter that Roger had been breaking the fucking law.

Her pulse screamed in her ears; Braylin wanted to break something, preferably on Blaze. She needed to talk to him about what happened between them and ask him to keep it to himself, but she was afraid if she opened her mouth right now, only words likely to go against that goal would come out.

Eyes narrowing, she contemplated climbing to a few hundred feet and dropping him out the side of the helicopter. Then there'd be no more Blaze to worry about messing up her reputation. It would at least get *one* of the stressors off her chest.

"I can feel you glaring at me," the smirky bastard drawled in a sleepy voice that set her heightened nerve endings abuzz for a whole different reason. *Damn him.* "If you need help, just ask."

Nope. She did not need help from him. Unless he offered to throw himself out of the aircraft at altitude. Braylin shook her head, they weren't even halfway through fire season, and she already needed a vacation.

With more grumbling, this time about lazy hotshots, she went back to working through her preflight checklist. If there were one thing that could calm her, it would be her regular routine. Taking a deep breath, she let it go, pushing everything else out of her mind to focus on ensuring the aircraft was safe for flight.

An hour later, they were airborne. Braylin had calmed down enough that she no longer wanted to send Blaze flying, but she felt far from settled. Her body vibrated with nervous energy. More than once, she'd opened her mouth to address the elephant in the cockpit only to chicken out and shut it again. They'd have to talk about Friday night at some point, but Braylin wasn't ready.

Blaze, in contrast, looked as relaxed as she was stressed. His fingers tapped a rhythm on his leg to the beat of some song only he could hear as he gazed out the window at the dense forest below.

How can he be so calm?

It infuriated her. Much like everything else about him. Braylin ground her teeth together and glared at the beautiful mountain landscape they flew over. A cloudless sky stretched beyond rocky peaks in the distance.

"Gorgeous day." Blaze's voice sounded over her headset, but she didn't respond.

The sky might be blue, but it felt as black as her mood. A thundercloud hung over her, and it was dark enough that she didn't know how she would get through a full day of training with Blaze.

Half tempted to turn the aircraft around with some maintenance excuse, Braylin's stomach dropped out of the bottom of the helicopter when the whine of the engine faded. Her gaze immediately flew to the instrument panel.

The 'engine out' light illuminated.

Not good.

She swallowed against the ball of fear stuck in her throat. They still had plenty of fuel, but the rotor blades were slowing down. To punctuate that point, the low rotor RPM warning horn sounded in her ears.

Fuck. Fuckity, fuck!

Her initial response was to panic as the engine completely quit on her, but she smothered it. Drumming up the emergency procedures for a situation like this, she repeated them in her head.

In the seat beside her Blaze clued into the fact something was wrong. "Braylin."

His voice barely penetrated as she punched the bucket with the button on the cyclic, unhooking it so it didn't get tangled up in anything as they autorotated down. Because they were going to crash. The question was how badly.

When visions of the bucket catching in a tree and sling-shotting the aircraft into the ground—a certified death sentence—flashed in her head, Braylin leaned into the side window, straining to ensure the hook had released. It had. As she watched the orange bucket shrink into a speck, relief teased her muscles into relaxing, but it was short-lived.

Goodbye, thousands of dollars of equipment. They weren't out of danger yet, and the cost of the water bucket was the least of her worries. Not only was the helicopter they flew in way more expensive, but she wasn't sure she could land them in one piece. It would be rough either way.

Her eyes scanned out the window for a spot not covered in trees that they could try to land in while she bottomed out the collective, lowering the pitch in the blades to get them moving again so they could glide down. Well, glide didn't really fit the hurtling she felt like they were doing . . . or maybe that was just her pulse.

"Are we going to crash?"

At the strain in his voice, Braylin glanced at Blaze. His hands gripped the seat cushion on either side of his legs, and the tan California boy had gone pale. He looked like how her insides felt, but she couldn't handle both of them panicking.

Instead of answering, she yelled, "Be quiet and strap in!"

She saw him reach for his lap belt and tighten it before she turned back to the terrain, scanning for a landing zone. As she searched, she keyed her radio, contacting the Forest Service dispatch to let them know she had to set down under an emergency.

In the seat beside her, she thought she heard Blaze utter an "Oh fuck," but she didn't have time to glance at him. The ground seemed to rise much—much—too quickly as they dropped toward it.

We might not have enough distance to land safely. Acknowledging that, her heart stopped in her chest and her throat closed up.

Though fear choked her, Braylin kept her wits about her and spotted a clearing covered in brush. It would be a tight fit for the blades, but it was the best she could do. Aiming toward it, she prayed to whoever would listen for them to come out of this alive.

As if in answer, the low rotor horn stopped its incessant screaming in her helmet as the blades regained RPM, rotating enough to slow their rate of descent and keep them from splattering on the side of the mountain.

Okay, you can do this.

Her world narrowed to their landing zone. The gorgeous day blurred around them until the only thing she could see was the blonde grasses of the clearing swaying in the breeze. Time moved in slow motion, but her thoughts sped.

She should've talked to Blaze, been nicer even. It wasn't his fault her past meant she was wary of relationships with men she worked with. She actually liked him, and he was a hell of a kisser. She should've told him.

Braylin blinked, and the litany of regrets stopped.

That's the fucking ground.

She eased back on the cyclic, lifting the nose of the helicopter to slow them down, and the sky filled the windscreen.

Blaze yelled her name at the sudden change in flight attitude.

"Trust me!" she yelled back, then pulled up on the collective to cushion the landing as she leveled the helicopter out. Even so, her eyes closed in reflex before they hit the ground, and she shouted, "Brace yourself!"

CHAPTER 8

The Aftermath

The world had become completely still, and the lack of motion froze Blaze's body into confusion. The sun's glare blurred his vision, adding to the fog holding him in stasis.

Where did the nightmare end and reality begin?

Slowly, a sound penetrated his haze. As if from a distance, a rapid beeping fired in his ears. He blinked a few times, and the interior of the cockpit came into focus through the sun visor on his flight helmet. What he could see looked . . . intact. For as hard as they'd hit the ground, he'd expected worse.

He lifted his arms to remove the helmet and stopped when a lightning bolt of pain struck his right shoulder. Wincing, Blaze probed gingerly with his left hand.

Shit. That didn't feel as it should.

He might not be a skilled paramedic, but he'd had emergency medical training to help out with accidents that occurred on the job. A year ago, one of the guys on his crew had dislocated his shoulder in a fall, and Blaze had reset it.

Adding pressure, he bit down on an oath as a wave of heat radiated from the spot. His gut told him he had a posterior dislocation.

Leaving his shoulder, he ran his hand over the rest of his body. Nothing else hurt; fingers and toes all worked like they should. Releasing a labored breath, he glanced over at Braylin.

Blaze's stomach hardened into a rock at the sight of her body angled forward across the cyclic.

Please let her be okay.

Unfastening his seat belt, he reached with his good arm and carefully tipped her back into her chair. Her eyes were closed behind the cracked plastic of her sun visor. He wasn't sure what she'd banged the helmet on when they landed, but he hoped the equipment did its job in protecting her head.

When he spoke her name, she didn't respond. A tremor of fear raced over his body, tightening his muscles into taut ropes.

Leaning down, Blaze placed his ear by her lips. Air brushed his skin, and he slumped in relief. She was breathing.

Lifting her broken visor, he pleaded, "Come on, angel. Open those pretty eyes for me."

The beeping he'd first heard grew louder. It came from her headset, but he didn't want to remove the helmet until he knew what her injuries were. Gently, he ran his hand over her like he'd done for himself.

He jumped when he got to her rib cage, and Braylin woke up with a sudden jerk.

Sweat broke out on her face as her breaths came in staccato pants. "What." Pant. "The." Pant. "Fuck?"

The gritted words made him want to kiss her. Shaky laughter bounced around his chest. If she were angry at him, she likely didn't have a head injury.

"Hello, gorgeous." Blaze's smile crept into his voice as relief turned his insides buoyant. "How are you feeling?"

"What?" She blinked, and her gaze darted around the cockpit. "We need to get out of here right now."

Taken aback by her urgency, he tried to get her

to calm down until he could make sure she was okay. "We will, but my shoulder's dislocated, and I need to know if you have any injuries."

"No! Out!" She undid her restraints, then unhooked the cord attached to her helmet. "Right now, Blaze. It's not safe." Her frantic fingers started to claw at the door handle.

"Geez, Braylin." The panic vibrating off her dragged him back into worry.

"Help me, dammit!"

Surprised at the desperation in her voice, Blaze leaned around her and pushed. As soon as the door opened, she hopped out with a grunted whimper that told him something pained her.

Shaking his head, he opened his side with his good arm and climbed out. Smoke choked him immediately, and he coughed at the acrid intrusion into his airways. Something was on fire, but his focus stayed on Braylin.

With stinging eyes, he met her on the other side of the helicopter. "Let me check you for . . ." He trailed off as he took in the scene before him.

The blades on the helicopter had long since stopped rotating, and flames expelled from the engine box.

Okay, so they might not get off the ground anytime soon, but at least the fire was a veritable smoke signal to their location. As long as it didn't spread to the trees ringing their clearing . . .

One problem at a time.

Braylin's face had turned ashen—in fear or pain—he wasn't sure. "This is really bad." Her words were little more than a whisper, and he almost missed them.

"Yeah, but hey. You landed us safely. We're *alive*." He emphasized the word, letting it soak in for himself, too.

We could've died.

Gulping, Blaze gripped her arm with his good side and forced her to look at him. "*You* did that, Braylin." He desperately wanted to kiss away the bewildered expression on her face. To show her how amazed he was by her, but he held back, knowing she wouldn't be receptive to it. Gentling his tone, he added, "Let me get our stuff. Then we'll figure the rest out."

"No!"

He'd already taken a step toward the helicopter, but the fear in her shout pulled him up short. Spinning around, he found Braylin clutching her arms over her middle, eyes wide and dark. "What is it?"

"You can't. The fire is almost to the fuel tank." She waved toward the helicopter like he didn't know where it was located. "We need to put distance between us and the aircraft." Gesturing for him to follow her, she shifted and grimaced.

Blaze frowned, and his thoughts raced. She'd injured something, and he needed to know how bad it was because watching her grimace in pain made his lungs too tight. Neither of them was in a condition to move anywhere quickly.

He studied the helicopter; he might be used to wildfires, but fire was fire. If you wanted to put it out, you starved it of fuel. The problem with this one was the *literal* fuel waiting to feed it in the tank. He tried to gauge the intensity and whether he'd have time to get to their stowed bags. The fire *was* spreading fast, the flames growing as the air fed them. The wind blew the smoke from them now, but the heat from it already reached where they stood ten feet away.

All their gear was still in the baggage compartment. If they just left it . . . losing his firefighting equipment would suck, but he could buy new stuff. What he didn't want to leave was their chance at getting off this mountain—sooner than later.

He'd stored his radio in his bag.

Cellphones were great when you had service, but he'd gotten used to working where there wasn't any. Because of that, he often left his phone stowed with his gear. Even if Braylin had hers, he doubted there'd be a signal in the middle of a mountain range. While he debated going for his equipment, the fire reached the fuel tank, and the flames spread, pushing him back a step from the force of their intensification.

Braylin must've sensed his hesitation because she grabbed his injured arm. He gritted his teeth against the ache that throbbed down it as she said, "Let's go! I don't want to be standing here if it shifts into the trees."

Staring at the pale green rimming her overly dark pupils, Blaze gave in. Even if he had time to grab the radio, putting her under more stress wasn't worth it. They'd been through enough for today.

"Okay, angel," he soothed. "Let's find a good rock for me to sit on while you play doctor."

* * *

Braylin ignored the pain in her ribs as they walked into the tree line beyond where she'd landed the aircraft. Her thoughts spun around the accident like a fire whirl. It had been way more horrifying than training to auto-rotate down in a simulator during flight school. Those moments where they'd been falling out of the sky still cramped her stomach in fear. But somehow, she'd managed it. They'd survived. Even so, she'd be happy never to repeat the experience.

Braylin took a deep breath to ease the wrench, tightening her insides, and felt a twinge before she blew it out. She must've rammed into the cyclic when they'd landed because her ribs were tender.

And Blaze. Had she really dislocated his shoulder?

Glancing at him, she noticed how he cradled his right arm to his chest and winced in sympathy.

At least we're alive.

Her mind returned to the moments when she'd thought they wouldn't be. She'd had regrets . . . about him. Watching his blonde waves swing as he strode beside her, Braylin sighed. She'd broken her rule and done the worst thing possible—developed feelings for the hotshot.

Too bad those *didn't die in the crash.*

Her mouth twisted with rueful humor. She might've kept Blaze alive on the landing, but she didn't need him burning himself to a crisp after the fact.

Thinking about his recklessness stirred her anger and tightened her hands into fists. Her gear had been stowed in the baggage compartment, too, but it wasn't worth the risk of third-degree burns or worse to retrieve it.

Shaking her head, she outpaced him, her steps becoming more of a stomp. The crash flashed again in her mind, and she frowned. The landing . . . she could've done better on it, but they *were* in one piece. An uncomfortable poke in her left side reminded her she wasn't without injury. The ache from her ribs persisted but muffled as if she flew through thick clouds.

We won't be flying anywhere soon.

A sigh collapsed her chest. When she'd come to and seen the 'engine fire' light on the instrument panel, she'd known they were in trouble. But . . .

What the heck happened?

The question niggled at her while the sounds of wildlife fleeing the damage behind them echoed through the trees. She didn't know what caused the fire or the crash. They'd had plenty of fuel, and she hadn't gotten any warning lights prior to the engine giving out.

It doesn't make sense.

She hadn't over-torqued it or exceeded any other limit, yet the damn thing quit on her. The idea to discuss it with Roger entered her mind and dragged her shoulders down.

Not an option anymore.

Not only had she lost the best crew chief she'd ever had, but now she'd lost the aircraft, too. Without any way to put the fire out, it would burn the helicopter to the ground. Her boss would flip his lid whenever he found out. *Whenever* that would be. They had no radio and no service for her cellphone.

A small part of her actually felt relief at the fact she didn't have a way to report the crash to her company. She'd like to put that tongue-lashing off for as long as possible.

But she had no idea how the hell they would get off this mountain.

They needed to get far enough away from the helicopter so they wouldn't be in the path of the fire's fuel should it spread to the trees, but the further they moved from the crash site, the harder it would be to get rescued. The Forest Service could see their last known location via the automated flight following in the aircraft. The clearing would be the first place they'd start searching.

Braylin slowed her steps. Blaze had been trailing her, and when he matched her stride, she stopped them. They'd only gone about fifty feet into the trees, but . . . "We should stay near the landing zone. It's the first place they'll look for us."

He glanced behind them, and she knew he was also worried about the fire moving into the trees. "Without a way to put the fire out . . ." He started to shrug, then groaned. Sweat broke out at his temples.

He was in way more pain than she was.

Guilt over being the cause strangled her voice as she demanded, "We need to fix your arm before we do anything else." Braylin reached for him as she asked, "You know how to do it?"

"Yeah." His gaze raked the forest, looking for something before he gave his head a shake and lowered to the ground. Propping his back against a tree trunk, he settled and managed a grin at her. "Ready to follow my orders, Nurse Whitney?"

Judging by the vise grip squeezing her gut, the answer was a definite "no." Her medical training began and ended with a first-aid kit. She had no clue how to put someone's arm back in its joint. The thought sent an uncomfortable skitter down her spine that she had to shake off.

You broke him. Now you have to fix him.

Staring into Blaze's blue eyes—bright, despite the pain—she shook her head at his cockiness and cleared the ball of fear from her throat. "Fine. Tell me what to do, doc."

* * *

Only half awake, Braylin snuggled into Blaze, listening to the sounds of a cozy fire crackling in the background. Her eyes remained closed, but her lips curved in a smile as his smoky scent penetrated. She lay there, content until the smell became overwhelming. Braylin didn't want to leave Blaze's side, but they must have fallen asleep too close to the fire because the fumes started to choke her.

She opened her eyes and bolted upright as her brain registered reality. They weren't cuddled together by the fireplace. Braylin stared up at the canopy of trees above their heads, and the blood drained out of her face. The noon-day sun would've blinded her, but a heavy layer of smoke filtered its rays.

The helicopter fire had spread.

Panic like she'd never felt rooted her body to the spot. Her eyes watched the embers dance in the treetops, lighting on leaves as they moved from branch to branch, and she couldn't look away. Her gaze flitted through them to the sliver of blue sky beyond the haze. She should be up *there* . . . not down here on the ground.

The ground. She was on the ground during a wildfire—with no way to escape.

That terrifying reality reverberated through her, and she clutched at her chest. Something was wrong with her heart. Or was it her lungs? She couldn't seem to catch her breath.

Am I having a heart attack?

The thought drifted slowly into her awareness, but her eyes stayed trained on the flames racing in their direction through the trees. She opened her mouth to call for Blaze, but nothing came out.

We survived the crash only to burn to death in the forest.

Now Braylin really couldn't breathe. She tried to stand, to move away from the blaze heading their way, but she ended up on all fours, wheezing for air. She'd rather have died in the crash. Burning to death had to be one of the worst ways to go.

"Braylin!"

Blaze pulled her to her feet, his injured arm escaping the makeshift sling they'd made from his belt after she'd helped reset it. He'd looked exhausted afterward, from the pain or something more, and they'd decided to sit and rest for a minute. But after what they'd been through, her body had shut down, too, and they'd fallen asleep.

It couldn't have been more than a couple of hours, but it had been long enough for the thing they'd feared to happen.

His gaze tracked the fire. "We have to run. Now."

"Can't," she gasped. "Can't breathe." Her heart slammed against her lungs, cutting off her air supply. "Heart," she wheezed, "attack."

He cupped her face and looked at her instead of the fire. "Yes, you can. You're not having a heart attack. You're hyperventilating."

She'd been trying to hold onto the cerulean tinge in his eyes when what he said penetrated. "What?" Indignation fired in her blood, and she stopped clutching uselessly at her chest. "I am not!"

She was *not* hyperventilating. One thing Braylin prided herself on was keeping a cool head. In the cockpit, she proved practically fearless. No way, she was having a panic attack. Sure, she'd panicked when the engine quit, but she'd set that shit aside and gotten the job done. This debilitating feeling was something new. And she didn't like it one bit. *No, sir!*

But Blaze didn't give her time to deal with whatever was or wasn't happening to her. His good hand reached for hers. "Then run!" He took off at a sprint, and she had no choice but to go with him.

She worked out on a regular basis and knew she was in pretty good shape, but her lungs couldn't seem to hold any oxygen. Not to mention, the pace Blaze set didn't help the pounding in her chest. Pretty soon, her heart would explode . . . at least then she wouldn't have to burn to death.

He dragged her uphill when she would rather have been heading *down* the mountain. Dust kicked up in their wake over the dry earth, but Braylin barely noticed. The tall bases of pine trees blurred in her peripheral vision as she half ran, half stumbled through the forest.

After several tortuous minutes, when she thought her legs would give out, they cleared the smoke, but she still couldn't pull in any air. Her lungs burned as though they were going up in flames, too.

She couldn't keep going. Her fingers slipped from Blaze's, and she crashed to the ground, bent over in a desperate attempt to inhale more than a few measly sips of air.

"Bla—" She tried to tell him, but her vision began graying at the edges. Her heartbeat jackhammered in her ears, and she didn't know where or how far he'd gone.

A strong hand rubbed her back, then his blonde locks came into view. "We're out of its path. Just breathe with me, okay?" Blaze placed one of her hands over her own diaphragm and the other palm over his. "Slow. Steady." His voice was a calming anchor amongst the waves of panic constricting her airways, and she held on to it to keep her surroundings from slipping away.

"Big deep breath in . . ."

Braylin wanted to argue about his treatment, but whatever he was doing seemed to be working. She inhaled with him, and her heart stopped racing.

"Good girl,"—he winked—"now, blow it back out."

If she could breathe, she'd tell him how his tone made her want to damage his favorite appendage. But she couldn't . . . yet, so she settled for a death glare.

After they repeated the process a few more times, she felt normal again and had had enough of his condescension. "Stop patronizing me or I'll knee you in the balls."

"Is that any way to say thank you?" He shook his head and tsked—*tsked*—at her.

She would punch him. Or worse . . . her gaze drifted to the smirk on his lips. When a part of her wanted to taste it, she crossed her arms and glowered at the laughter dancing in his eyes. Better to be angry than vulnerable.

She didn't need their situation to become any more complicated, and sex—after she'd told him it was never going to happen again—would definitely complicate it. Best to remember he was a cocky playboy. The type of man she wanted nothing to do with.

Braylin dropped her arms, tracing the seam of the utility knife in her flight suit pocket, and shot him a smile with a dangerous edge. "I can think of other ways."

If he didn't die from the fire, it'd be a miracle if he made it off this mountain unscathed.

CHAPTER 9

Hunger & Thirst

"So, what now?" The fact she even needed to ask that question left a sour taste on Braylin's tongue. Though she had her breathing under control, humiliation slithered just under her skin, threatening to rear its ugly head if she didn't think about something else and fast. She didn't like not being in charge, but on the ground during a fire, let's face it, *this* was Blaze's territory—not hers.

His eyes shuttered as if lost in thought. His arms hung by his sides, and she worried about the injured one not being supported. The belt they'd used to secure it lay useless at a diagonal across his chest. For some reason, the look made her think of Indiana Jones. But being lost in the mountains wasn't her idea of an adventure, no matter how sexy her co-star looked.

Braylin didn't want to know what *she* looked like after all they'd been through today, but Blaze managed to look like he always did—ruggedly disheveled—like he'd just walked off the beach. She wondered what the stubble on his face would look like after he couldn't shave it for a few days . . . or what it'd *feel* like.

Not helpful!

Braylin gave herself a mental slap. That was the opposite of what she needed to think about right now.

She'd been in this situation before. Lost, trekking through the wilderness, and wishing for a rescue. It had been a part of her military training, but she'd hoped never to repeat the experience. All Army pilots had to go through SERE—Survival, Evasion, Resistance, and Escape—school. Though she could be thankful she and Blaze weren't behind enemy lines to worry about the resistance and escape part, they still had to survive and evade the freaking fire they started.

Blaze's eyes cleared and focused on her. "It's unusual, but the wind is blowing the fire downhill. Our best bet is to head uphill and away from it."

Just one problem with that . . . Braylin

propped her hands on her hips and raised a brow. "But since any rescue asset won't be able to find us at the crash site, I'd rather head *down* the mountain. You know . . . to a road?"

"Yeah." Blaze shot her a grin that alternately heated her blood and chilled her to the bone. She had a feeling she wouldn't like whatever he said next. "So we go up and over to get back *down*."

She tried and failed to hide the whine that left her throat. The further they climbed away from the crash site, the less likely they'd be found, which meant locating a road and getting back to civilization on their own.

Oh, goodie.

She didn't know how long that process might take. Braylin gazed out through the pines, aspens, and spruces, but all she saw were *more* trees. Just how far were they from the peak? It could take a day or more to climb it. They needed to find water and food if they were going to make it that long. She had a granola bar in her flight suit, but that would hardly sustain both of them for any length of time if they had to hike Mount Everest here.

With a sigh that felt as heavy as she knew the dark would be when it fell, she waved Blaze ahead of her. "All right, hotshot. Lead the way."

* * *

Even without his helmet, sweat dripped down Blaze's forehead, and he wiped it away with the back of his forearm. He'd rolled up the sleeves of his yellow Nomex shirt, but with the afternoon sun beating down on them as they climbed, it provided little relief from the high summer temps. It didn't help he could practically feel Braylin's angry stare boring into his back and figured the heat in it would be hot enough to sear his skin if they were closer.

They'd been walking in silence for the last two hours, and he kept waiting to hear her ask him to stop. He'd set a pace that had his own lungs working hard, but so far, every time he glanced behind him to make sure she kept up with him, Braylin was right there, shooting him a look that warned him not to open his mouth. The thought made his lips twitch in a smirk.

Since she'd had her panic attack, Braylin became extra prickly. He understood it had freaked her out. She was so used to being in control that kind of weakness scared her in more ways than one.

Blaze shook his head. The woman needed to realize he wouldn't rub that in her face. Hell, he'd panicked when the helicopter was going down, but she'd been imperturbable then. Everyone had their strengths and weaknesses, and no one was perfect.

A sigh lifted his shoulders.

But Miss Strung-Tight-as-a-Bow behind him didn't get that memo, apparently.

He didn't like it, but he understood. They were in a stressful situation. Just because they were moving in the opposite direction of the fire didn't mean they were safe. The winds could shift uphill at any time, and they'd be on the run again. He'd seen that happen more than once in his last five years as a wildland firefighter.

Of course, it made things worse that they had no way of remedying the watch-out situation they were in either. 'No communication link' was one of the 18 watch-outs on a fire, and unfortunately, they were without a radio or a cell tower, which meant they had no way to contact their crew or supervisors.

Not having a radio or his tools wasn't ideal, but Blaze had every confidence they'd get off this mountain alive. And he didn't mind having the extra alone time with Braylin until then.

As soon as she decided to quit being mad at him, that is.

Turning his head on a slight angle, he caught

sight of her red cheeks and knew she had to be tiring. He trained for this kind of hike as part of his job, and even he felt ready for a break. They'd have to stop soon anyway and find some water if they didn't want to get dehydrated.

Watching her out of the corner of his eye, he thought he heard a whimper, but she quickly replaced it with a scowl. This climb would be challenging under normal conditions, and being injured . . . A misstep caused Blaze to grimace. He'd placed his arm back in the sling they'd made, but he felt it with every uneven section of elevation.

Pulling his eyes away from her, Blaze focused on the ground before he wound up losing his footing. He'd surely eat dirt with one of his arms bound. The only good that would come of a fall would be Braylin laughing at him. Maybe then she'd loosen up a little. He wished she would because he'd prefer to go back to the playful snapping instead of her wanting to bite his head off simply for breathing.

The tension between them had ratcheted up several notches, and not all of that resulted from their current situation. He wanted to ask her about Friday night, figure out what she'd been upset about before they'd ended up in that storeroom. Maybe when they stopped for a rest, he'd broach the subject. Since she was already pissed at him, he didn't see the harm in asking.

With a smile that had a hint of mischief in it, Blaze inhaled, and the scents of the forest entered his nose. Pine proved the predominant smell, but he got a whiff of damp earth and eyed the ground more closely. The musty odor alerted him to the fact there had to be a stream nearby. He slowed to tell Braylin, but she was no longer right behind him. Whirling, Blaze saw her cutting across the forest.

Where is she going? "Braylin!"

She turned at his call with a huff, propping her hands on her waist. Every time she did that, his eyes fell on the shape of her hips, and he admired the way the stance pulled the fabric of her flight suit tight to her body. He was curious why she hadn't taken the suit off. She had to be hot.

His blood heated when his brain supplied the response that she must not be wearing anything underneath it. He would love to find out because he wanted to put his hands on those curves again.

"There's water this way. Hurry up."

Blaze blinked, and what she'd said penetrated the fantasy his mind had slipped into.

Should've known. Internally, he shook his

head at himself while he picked up his pace to catch her. When he'd reached her, he asked, "And you know this how?"

Her response was a mutter that sounded like 'sear'. "What was that?"

She sighed, and though she walked in front of him, he felt the accompanying eye roll. "SERE. Survival training. All military pilots have to go through it."

Oh shit. *SERE*. He'd heard of *that* . . . but he thought it was only something special forces guys had to do.

Wow. Her toughness had already impressed him, but knowing she'd made it through that kind of training gave Blaze a whole new level of respect for her.

"That's hella cool." He couldn't hide the note of awe in his voice.

Her steps slowed, and she gave him the strangest look before mumbling, "Thanks." Her eyes held more gray than he'd ever seen in them. It swirled into and out of the bits of green and brown. He had no clue what it meant.

Hell, if he didn't know any better, he'd think his comment embarrassed her. *Interesting* . . . "How long were you in the military?"

"I did five years with the Army." She kept

heading toward the source of water, but at least she answered him.

"As a helicopter pilot?"

"Yep."

He'd figured but was done with making assumptions about her. "Why'd you get out?"

Though subtle, he didn't miss the way her steps faltered and her shoulders tensed at the question. He'd hit a nerve with that one.

"What is this? Twenty questions?" Braylin's voice sounded a little too unruffled when she turned on him with a smirk. "If so, it's your turn to answer one."

Since she'd stopped walking, he did the same. His shoulder instantly thanked him when the jarring he'd felt with each step ended.

Watching her try to play it off, he bit back a smile. Talking was better than angry silence, so he'd let that one go . . . for now. "Angel, you can ask me as many questions as you want."

"Do you have any food?"

A laugh burst from Blaze's lips. She did *not* go in the direction he'd been expecting her to. "I think I have a power bar. Why?"

"Because if we don't make it off this mountain today, we'll need something to eat, and all I have is a single granola bar." She crossed her arms and stared him down, but he had no clue what she was waiting for.

When he caught on, he started patting his pockets. Sure enough, he'd left a protein bar in his pants. Pulling it out, Blaze offered, "I'll share as long as you're not allergic to peanut butter."

She uncrossed her arms. "I'm not, but save it 'til we find some water." Without another word, she spun away and started heading toward what he hoped was a clean source they could drink from.

Conversation over. He read her message loud and clear. Braylin had some high walls, but that was okay. He liked a good climb . . . besides, he bet the reward would be worth the effort it took to scale them.

* * *

Braylin had found a creek, and they both dove at it like it was a fountain in the Sahara. The water barely trickled over a rocky bed, but it was something. Cupping a hand, Blaze lifted it to his lips.

Tepid. But drinkable.

As they drank, birds chirped on their flight through the trees while the noises of insects buzzed all around them. Here, life persisted despite the drought this area had been experiencing. Blaze finished, then splashed water on his face in an attempt to cool down. It didn't work. Especially when he glanced over and caught sight of Braylin's lacy blue bra through the gap in her button-up work shirt. She'd finally unzipped her flight suit and had the arms knotted around her waist. He hadn't figured her for a lace kind of gal, but it was just one more detail about her he wanted to learn.

When she splashed water on her neck and closed her eyes, he had a vision of them in the shower together. After they made it off this mountain, that was going to happen. She rubbed more liquid on her neck and chest; Blaze couldn't look away. His eyes trailed a droplet as it dripped between the valley of her breasts. He wanted to lick it off. Badly.

His body reacted, and his blood rushed south. She might still be angry with him, but it had to be a cover for something else. Fear or a past hurt? While they were on this mountain, he was determined to find out.

Because after he did and she finally let go, he was going to lick every inch of her. Go slow; let the fire build where before they'd given it too much fuel too fast. Blaze was seconds away from closing the distance between them and taking a kiss from those caustic lips when a familiar roar penetrated his fantasy.

Braylin's eyes flew open, and she surged to her feet. "A helicopter!"

He rose more slowly, careful of his injured arm.

"It's a Blackhawk." Braylin searched the sky in a frantic motion, looking for the chopper. "Damn, I wish we had a flare or—" Her eyes snapped to him. "Take off your shirt!"

"What?" He struggled to keep up with her train of thought.

"It's the brightest thing we have!" She gripped the front and started pulling at the buttons. "We'll use it to signal the aircraft."

Blaze tried to shoo her hands away so he could do as she asked, but she wasn't having it. While she worked the buttons, he undid his sling instead. As soon as she'd gotten the top few undone, he reached back and pulled the over-shirt off. Once she held it in her hands, Braylin started waving it like a madwoman.

"Do you see the helicopter? It's got to be a search and rescue craft."

Blaze searched the sky. The noise had continued to grow, so it had to be getting closer.

The tree cover was denser near the creek, and without a panel, he didn't hold much hope of it seeing them. But he wasn't going to tell *her* that.

"There!" The Blackhawk came into view, and Blaze pointed.

Braylin spotted it and started waving his shirt like a flag girl at the Olympics. He added his good arm to the show, even if a small part of him didn't actually want the helicopter to see them.

Because he wasn't ready for this time they had together, to end.

CHAPTER 10

That's not Bullwinkle

Watching the helicopter fly away, completely oblivious to their attempts to hail it, snapped something inside Braylin. The dam holding in her frustration burst, carried by a wave of fear she'd been staunching, and she felt the deluge coming up and out of her mouth with little hope of stopping it.

She whirled on her target. "I swear to God, Blaze. You are like my own personal Murphy's law. You know how many crashes I'd been in before this one?" Without waiting for an answer, she chucked the useless shirt at him.

His calm stare didn't waver, which only raised the level of her ire.

Gritting her teeth, she ground out, "Zip. Zilch.

Ze-ro.”

He shot her that playboy smile. “Oh, come on, Bray. You can't blame me for the crash. That's crazy talk.”

That was *so* the wrong thing to say to her. Her blood pressure spiked, and she got in his face. From the outside, it might've looked comical, considering he had several inches on her height, but she didn't care right now. “Do not call me Bray or crazy unless you want my knife embedded in your gut, clear?”

His smile shifted into a smolder, and his voice dropped its teasing tone. “I don't know why, but you threatening me is a huge turn-on.”

Rather than admit the delicious pull she felt at his words, Braylin went on the defensive. “You sick, twisted, son of a—”

Blaze's mouth cut off her insult, and for the briefest of seconds, she let herself enjoy the kiss. That same liquid warmth entered her veins like a soothing river.

But then sanity returned, and she shoved hard on his chest, pushing him away. “Asshole!”

Let him think her labored breathing came from anger, not how heated that one little kiss made her.

Blaze didn't respond; he wasn't even looking

at her. More than a little miffed, Braylin huffed out a breath, turning to see what held him so transfixed.

Oh, wow.

"Walk backward. Slowly." Blaze's warning floated over her head, soft and calm as she stared at the moose across the creek from them.

"I've never seen one in person. They're huge!" The animal had to be seven feet tall at the shoulder. Awe widened her eyes and sent a rush of adrenaline tingling through her body. A part of her wanted to pet it. What would its coat feel like?

Blaze was not on the same page. Behind her, he whisper-shouted, "And dangerous! Back away. Slowly."

The moose's head turned in their direction and became very still.

"Now, Braylin!" The last shred of calm fled from Blaze's voice as he growled the command at her.

She didn't know what he was so worried about. Weren't moose just like . . . oversized deer? "It's probably more afraid of us than we are of it." Thinking the thing would take off as soon as she took a step toward it, Braylin ignored Blaze's order and moved forward. "I bet it'll just run aw—"

Uh-oh.

The hair on the back of the moose's neck rose. She could see it from twenty feet away, standing in a line of dark brown fur beyond the largest rack of antlers she'd ever seen.

"Dammit, Braylin!" He grabbed her hand and started to tug her backward. She heard him mutter, "And you claim *I* never listen," before he squeezed her hand and commanded, "If that thing charges us, run like hell until you can find a rock or a tree to hide behind."

Is he serious?

But she didn't need Blaze to answer. The moose's ears went back, then it grunted at them and stomped its feet.

"It seems agitated," she whispered, fear flooding in and replacing the awe she'd first felt. Her legs trembled, desperate to run, but Blaze held her steady with his hand in hers. At a snail's pace, they backed away.

Braylin's eyes stayed glued on the moose. The hairs on its hump didn't lower, and it kept grunting at them. They were maybe thirty feet away when her heel caught in a tree root, and she stumbled, taking Blaze down with her. An involuntary screech left her lips as she fell, and once she'd hit the ground, every muscle in her body seized as tight as if she'd been tased.

Lifting her head with a snap, Braylin knew what she'd find. The moose kicked its front hooves out at them . . . then charged.

"Fuck!" Blaze pulled her to her feet, but her eyes were locked on the moose. "Run, Braylin!"

He didn't drop her hand as he sprang into a sprint. Her head whipped around, and her feet followed as they raced against the angry animal. At first, she heard it crashing through the trees behind them, but then her world narrowed to the sounds of her body.

Adrenaline kept her heart rate pumping as loud as helicopter blades whacking the air. Her breaths were short, quick expulsions punctuated by the constant thumping of her pulse in her ears. Trees flew by in a blur of brown and green as she ran blindly with no thought to direction. She hoped Blaze knew where they were going and that it wasn't down the mountain.

If someone had told her this was how her day would've gone, she'd have laughed at the absurdity of it, knowing it couldn't possibly be true. She'd been in a crash, had to flee a wildfire, and now a giant moose wanted to stomp her to death.

What in the world did I do to piss off the

powers that be so badly?

"Whoa!" All of a sudden, her forward momentum halted with a swift jerk to the left. Blaze pulled her behind a giant juniper, placing a finger on his lips in the universal sign for 'quiet'.

The tree's conical shape provided ten feet of spread for them to hide under. Braylin tried to quiet her panting breaths as they waited against the branches for the moose to run by . . . or sniff them out. Could moose do that? She had no idea what kind of hunting senses they had. Worrying about it, she unconsciously squeezed Blaze's hand as tight as she could.

Please let it pass us by.

A moment later, the moose rushed past their tree, crashing through low-hanging boughs with its antlers and sending leaves flying. She sucked in a sharp breath, waiting.

But it didn't stop.

Relief sucker punched her, and all her saved breath rushed out. "Thank God!"

Noticing she had a death grip on Blaze's hand, Braylin dropped it so fast you'd think it scalded her. On wobbly legs, she turned to him, unsure what to say other than . . . "I'm sorry."

* * *

Is she actually apologizing?

The pallor of Braylin's face told Blaze she felt genuinely sorry. But was she apologizing for unloading on him, not listening about the moose, or both?

It didn't matter. He wasn't upset about either of those things.

She'd been snapping at him since they'd met, and with the stress they were under, he felt relieved she'd finally let some of it loose. As for the moose, he'd heard horror stories about run-ins with them from guys on his crew. It didn't take much for a moose to feel harassed, and this one had probably been agitated by the chopper noise. A couple of years ago, he'd seen a small group of them from a distance while on a fire, but until today, he'd been lucky enough to avoid that particular animal.

Even though regret swam in Braylin's eyes, some part of him couldn't help poking at her. He flexed his fingers and asked, "For nearly breaking the bones in my hand?"

That wiped the look of repentance from her face like he'd known it would. Now, the green in those mood-ring eyes swirled. "You just can't help it, can you?"

"Help what?"

She crossed her arms and cocked out a hip. "Being an asshole."

A laugh burst from his chest, but when he saw no trace of humor in her expression, Blaze sobered. With a sigh, he gave her a truth. "It's a defense mechanism."

A quick flicker of revelation in her eyes before they slid away, and she murmured, "Guess we have something in common after all."

It was his turn to be surprised. Not that her abrasiveness was a shield—that he'd known—but the fact she'd been willing to admit it to him. A spark of hope lit within Blaze, and he stretched out a hand. "How about a truce?"

Braylin managed to smirk. "I didn't realize we were at war."

Nice one, angel.

Withdrawing the palm she didn't want to take; Blaze gestured between them. "So this past week has been, what, friendly fire?"

"No." A taunting shake of her head. "We aren't friends."

She might've meant it teasingly, but the barb struck true, lodging itself in his chest with enough force to smother the spark of hope he'd felt. He tried not to let his disappointment color his voice when he said, "You've made that clear."

A line cut between her brows. "I don't want to like you."

"Ah," the spark reignited, and a grin split Blaze's lips before he added, "That means you do."

She scoffed, hinting at her exasperation. "It *means* we're stuck with each other until we find a way off this mountain or get rescued. And I don't have the energy to climb all day *and* fight with you."

Sure, she doesn't.

Maybe it was the adrenaline still charging through his veins from fleeing the moose, or that flicker of hope he wanted to fuel, but a need to answer the unspoken challenge in her words narrowed his focus to the kiss he'd stolen. It played on repeat in his head.

Craving another one, Blaze stepped toward her until they were nearly chest-to-chest. "I enjoy arguing with you, Braylin." When she tilted her chin to meet his gaze, he added, "And watching the colors in your eyes go sharp."

She didn't back up, so he dipped his head. Desire slashed at his throat, and his voice rasped. "But I think that fire works even better when we use it for this."

A chocolate strand of hair had escaped her ponytail and lay across her cheek. Blaze brushed it off, then trailed his thumb along all that smooth skin toward her mouth. A soft breath escaped her waiting lips as he leaned in closer. When those hazel eyes turned the foggy brown of arousal, a burn licked at his blood in response, like throwing fresh kindling on a fire.

But he'd already crossed the line once today, taking what hadn't been offered. This time, it would be her choice.

"Your move," Blaze spoke the words so low they were barely more than a rumble of air fluttering across her half-closed lids.

A breath apart, he waited, drinking in her scent. That heady mixture of lavender and vanilla managed to override the smells of the forest around them. Soft and sweet. Two things she'd yet to be with him.

Come on, angel.

The seconds stretched until he thought she'd leave him hanging. But then her eyes closed, her body shifting into his. The slightest lean but enough to mean she'd given in. A moment later, Braylin's mouth met his.

Blaze's inner voice screamed hallelujah while his insides combusted. She had the power to affect him like no one had before, not even Sloane. Considering that most of the time he'd spent with

Braylin had been in arguments, something had to be wrong with him. Was he a closet masochist? Or maybe because his sparring with Braylin was the polar opposite of his last real relationship was what made it so appealing.

When Braylin's tongue teased at his lips, Blaze changed the angle of the kiss, giving her more access. Despite the tangle of tongues, there was no urgency this time, no desperation—just a mutual exploration.

They tested and tasted. Learning flavors and pleasure points. He probably used his injured arm more than he should, but he couldn't *not* hold her. Cupping her face in his palms, he savored her lips. Here, she was sweet with a trace of the creek's earthiness. Then he trailed his thumbs across the skin of her neck. There, a faint moan when he touched behind her left ear.

At the sound, a desperate need clawed its way to the surface, and he nibbled her bottom lip. When she responded with a hungry gasp, Blaze lost himself in studying her. Seconds, minutes, time ceased to exist while he memorized everything that made her melt into his arms.

When they finally separated, he lowered his forehead to hers, both breathing hard, and it had nothing to do with the altitude. He was on fire for her after one kiss.

Blaze lifted his forehead without releasing her face because he didn't want to let go. "Way better than fighting."

The brown in her eyes was almost gold. A new color, making him wonder what it meant. As he held her, a slow smile started in them, then spread across her face. It took his breath away.

My angel.

Blaze didn't question the thought. He needed her to be his and no one else's. His blood was so hot for her the wild part of him wanted to fuck her up against a tree in broad daylight. As if he could mark her—claim her—the way an animal might. But whatever burned between them was more complicated than that.

So he held that part of himself in check. Their next time would be slow. An odyssey of her body. That's what she deserved, and that's what he'd give her . . . whenever she was ready.

CHAPTER 11

Blowing Hot & Cold

For the second time in as many minutes, Braylin stumbled against the uneven ground. They were following the creek up the mountain. The water burbled in the background of her awareness as it traveled over the rocky bed it had carved into the mountainside. Though her eyes watched her footing, she didn't see the obstructions in her path. Rocks and fallen twigs became eager hands reaching through the earth to grab at her heels while her vision turned inward to the kiss she'd shared with Blaze.

I'm so weak.

She'd given in when she should've been stronger—should've resisted.

She'd said nothing afterward. Noth-ing. It was

like his mouth had turned her brain to mush, and all she'd been able to do was smile at him. He probably thought that meant she wanted to do it again. And well, she did. But she wouldn't.

Right?

Because they worked together, *and* he gave off total player vibes. While the idea of enemies with benefits had an appeal, she couldn't lie to herself. That's not what it would be with him. She *liked* Blaze. And even if they could be friends with benefits, she didn't trust herself not to want more.

That truth pulled her lips into a frown. The hotshot had gotten under her skin. She wasn't sure yet if that was good or bad, but it had to be dangerous.

What is it about him?

She envied his carefree attitude, and despite his methods, he had shown he was capable of compassion when he'd helped her with her— *sigh*—panic attack. She choked on the words. *Panic attack.*

She'd never had one before, and she hoped she never did again because not only was it scary as hell . . . it was beyond embarrassing. The whole morning, she'd been waiting for him to rub it in her face.

But he hadn't.

Instead, he'd saved her from a crazy moose and then kissed her until she melted into a puddle at his feet. Like some supplicant worshiping the sex god that had the power to make her relinquish control and be blissfully happy about it.

She snorted. Maybe the high summer sun was getting to her because that seemed ridiculous . . . but, my God, the man could kiss.

Braylin sucked her bottom lip between her teeth; Blaze's smoky, salty flavor lingered there. She remembered how he'd nibbled on it and how that had sent an electric current straight to her lady bits. They still buzzed with need.

A pebble rolled under her boot, sending her wobbling a couple of steps before she caught herself. "Dammit!"

"You okay back there, angel?" Blaze called over his shoulder.

"Fine!" Braylin snapped as heat crept up her neck. He didn't need to know why she couldn't seem to walk straight.

He chuckled in response as if he could read her thoughts, and her eyes narrowed on the back of his dingy yellow shirt. She might be starting to like him, but that didn't mean he couldn't still irritate her.

Cocky bastard.

The words didn't hold any wrath now, even in her head. Part of her wanted to know what had made him start using cockiness as a defense mechanism because she knew all about putting up a front to keep from getting hurt.

Memories of her ex tried to crowd in, but Braylin pushed them away.

Who or what had hurt Blaze?

I could *ask.*

She definitely wanted to. But that would mean telling her own sob story in return, and she wasn't ready to trust him with that. While she contemplated it, her stomach twisted with her thoughts. They'd shared her granola bar where they'd first stopped at the creek, and now it became a knot, adding to the unsettled feeling in her insides. All the stress was probably giving her an ulcer.

Rubbing a hand on her middle as if that could soothe it, Braylin tensed more at Blaze's shout. Her head snapped up, but it was more of a whoop than anything intelligible as he took off at a sprint. He disappeared, and she realized the elevation changed, dropping down after so much climbing. Tired, sweaty, and sore, she wasn't about to run after him. Whatever he'd gotten excited about, she'd find out eventually.

* * *

The tree cover ended as the creek opened into an alpine lake. Blaze charged forward, care over his injured shoulder forgotten. His first instinct was to jump in—clothes and all. At this elevation, the temperature had to be cooler than the water they'd drunk. He figured they were somewhere near 10,000 feet by now, which meant snowmelt likely fed the lake. His eyes traced the bowl carved into the landscape below a ridge of craggy peaks. It was—in a word—idyllic.

Turning around to see if Braylin wanted to join him for a swim, he had a moment of panic when she wasn't there, but then her head crested the top of the rise. He smiled and waved as the clamp that had gripped his chest released. They might both be well-matched for their situation, but he couldn't help but feel protective of her.

Though they'd been through a lot today already, the mountain could throw so many more things at them. The helicopter fire was the most pressing concern, but there was always a chance of snake bites or running into other unfriendly animals.

Blaze shook off the worry over things he had no control over and watched Braylin as she carefully picked her way down the rocky slide. To either side, the gravel fanned out into green grass split here and there by hardy wildflowers. Yellow, white, and pink blooms stood tall, unimpeded by anything but stray clouds as they soaked up the sunshine.

If it had been a different day, he could imagine they'd hiked in to picnic by the lake for the afternoon—on a date. And since they were alone in a secluded spot, he'd have seduced her here, under a sky aflame with the sunset before it faded into night.

The vision was so clear that when he blinked it free, the too-bright afternoon rays made him frown. A twinge of anxiety gripped his lungs, and he scrubbed a hand across his chest at the unfamiliar sensation. Worry tightened the pressure against them as if he might not ever get the chance to take Braylin out. Would she let him when they made it off this mountain?

He admired what little he knew of her but wanted to learn the rest. So far, she'd proven to be very different from his ex-girlfriend. He couldn't imagine Sloane keeping pace with him as they trekked up a mountain. The outdoors had not been her thing, and she would probably have asked to be carried within the first fifteen minutes.

But not Braylin. She'd shown she was both tough and capable, but he wondered how much of her prickliness was truly her personality or only a way to protect herself. While he didn't want to coddle her, he did want the chance to show her what being treasured felt like. Something told him that would be a new experience for her.

Hope that she might let him sputtered to life in his chest again.

On instinct, he walked to the nearest patch of wildflowers, plucking a few of the deep pink blooms. He smirked down at them once he held them in his hands. Up close, they were almost purple, and he immediately knew what they were—fireweed.

The plant had the nickname because it liked to grow in places ravaged by fire. Blaze's stomach quivered as he stared down at them. He hoped the wildfire the crash created stayed away from their location. He'd checked the weather every so often on the climb, but the wind still worked in their favor to blow it in the opposite direction. Silently, he begged Mother Nature to keep it that way.

Clutching his bouquet, Blaze joined Braylin, where she'd stopped at the bottom of the hill.

Raising a brow as she accepted his offering,

she asked, "What is this for?"

Suddenly self-conscious over the gesture, the asshole part of him said, "Well, I wouldn't eat them. They're toxic."

Her eyes widened a little before she glared at him. "You gave me poisonous flowers?"

"No! I mean, yes." Unfamiliar emotions had him stumbling over his words, and he scrubbed a hand at the back of his neck. "I just . . . thought they were pretty and wanted you to have them."

You're a fucking idiot, Blaze. At this moment, he felt a lot more like Noah, the easy bravado he'd always worn as Blaze just beyond his frantic grasp.

Whatever had possessed him to give her the flowers had clearly been a bad idea. She stared at him like he'd grown a second head. The longer her gaze bored into him, the more uncomfortable he became. Fresh sweat broke out at his temples. The kind that came from fear, not the heat of the sun.

Her eyes swirled with green, brown, and light blue until he had no clue what she was thinking. A lump the size of the rocks around them formed in Blaze's throat while he waited for her to say something . . . anything!

"Thank you." She didn't smile with the comment, and despite the solid ground, he felt unsure of his footing.

Shit! Do I say, 'You're welcome,' or is that asinine?

Braylin stopped his mental breakdown by walking away. She knelt on the grass at the lake's edge and dipped her hand into the water. "It might be too cold to swim, but I'd like to try."

Beads of perspiration dripped down Blaze's back. "Yeah, I think it's fed by snowmelt, but that was my first thought too."

"Really, Blaze. No crack about skinny dipping?" When she grinned over her shoulder, his body relaxed, letting go of the tension their weird exchange had caused.

He shot her a wink. "I'm game if you are."

* * *

W. T. F.?

Blaze had given her flowers.

How am I supposed to keep resisting him when he does something sweet like that?

She couldn't remember the last time a man had given her flowers. Her stomach cramped as if to prove that wasn't true. Well, the last time was probably Rob. A gift for whatever holiday they'd spent together last. He'd always given her a dozen red roses, never bothering to learn that they were her least favorite bloom . . . but she preferred not to dwell on those memories. After her world had fallen apart, she'd taken a knife and cut that time with him, that year, out of her life. Stored it away in a box she never opened, wishing she could get rid of it altogether.

Frigid drops of water smacked her in the face, and she gasped, pulled out of the rabbit hole her mind had dragged her down. Mouth set in a determined line, Braylin cupped chilly water in her palms and tossed it back at Blaze. "Asshole!"

"Fuck, that's cold!" Her throw hit him smack in the middle of his bare chest.

Braylin laughed as he flinched against the bracing temperature of the lake water. "Yes, it is!"

Her nipples were hard points behind her bra. They'd stripped down to their underwear, but she'd only been joking about the skinny dipping. She knew where that would lead.

Staring at Blaze's chest, she tried not to drool over the muscles that were so sharp they could've been painted on. He was tall and cut. Not bulky like someone who lifted weights at the gym but strong in all the right places. His biceps came from digging line, his back and chest muscles from carrying heavy equipment around, and the definition in his abs from climbing at high altitudes. She hadn't really appreciated them that night in the storage closet.

I've never done it in a lake before . . .

Nope! Braylin cut off those thoughts as soon as they started. There was absolutely no getting naked around Blaze.

His kiss would warm her up. *Double nope!*

Exercise would warm her up, too. Pushing off the pebbles worn smooth by the water on the bottom of the lakebed, Braylin cut across the near crystal-clear surface, swimming with sure strokes to the deeper side—away from Blaze. When she reached a depth where she couldn't touch the bottom, she treaded water, trying not to shiver at the cold permeating everything up to her chin. After another few minutes, she'd be ready to get out.

She tilted her head back and nearly gasped as the cool water touched her ears and cheeks. The sky was a bright blue, a shade lighter than Blaze's eyes. That made Braylin scoff at herself, annoyed that she couldn't look at the sky without thinking of him.

Needing more distance, she swam further into the deeper end of the lake, but every stroke seemed to push colder and colder water into her face. Her teeth chattered against each other by the time she heard Blaze's shouts. Turning toward his call, she saw him cutting a path toward her.

"Are you crazy?" It was nearly a growl when he reached her. "The further in you go, the colder the water will be. Do you *want* hypothermia?"

The question was clearly rhetorical as he continued to rant about the normal human body temperature and the effects of prolonged cold exposure. While he blustered at her, he rubbed her arms as if that would make her any warmer, floating in frigid water.

She would've bristled if she hadn't recognized the condescension for what it was—concern. "I am a, a lit-tle col-d." A shiver racked her while she chattered the words out. Maybe she had gone a bit too far into the water.

Blaze's face had never looked so stern before. A deep line marred his forehead. "Can you swim back? It'll help you warm up."

"Ye-ess." She nodded in case her shivering made that unintelligible.

A sharp nod. "Good. Let's go."

He swam to her side, and she started to butterfly back. When she lifted her head after a pull, her eye caught on Blaze, keeping pace with her. Her muscles already felt warmer, and the competitive part of her wanted to see if she could smoke him. Grinning internally, Braylin pushed herself, surging farther with each stroke until she could see the pebbles on the bottom of the lake. Knowing they'd reached the shallow end, she stopped and spun to see Blaze a length behind her.

Satisfaction made her smirk, though her face felt numb, and she wasn't sure she pulled the look off. "I w-win," she told him when he finally made it to her side.

"I didn't realize it was a race." Blaze shot her a rueful smile as he stood, slicking the hair back from his face. He could reach the bottom where they'd stopped, but she couldn't.

Though the temperature leaned toward frigid, she wasn't ready to get out yet. It had felt so good to wash off the day they'd had. Not just the sweat and dirt but the fear and stress that had seemed like a layer all on its own.

He moved toward the beach, stopping in knee-deep water, probably because she hadn't followed him. When he turned, Braylin tried not to drool. His plaid boxers were plastered to his body . . . every toned, wet inch of him.

Isn't the cold supposed to shrink it?

She blinked when he appeared in front of her. His knuckle rubbed against her bottom lip, and she felt a moment of dread that she had—in fact—been drooling, but he only said, "You're blue."

Relief washed over her like the water she still treaded. "So, are yo-uu."

Heat sparked in his eyes as he drew even closer, pushing her further into the lake until it reached his pecs. "Still cold?"

She could only nod as he grasped her legs and wrapped them around his waist. "Me too." Then he dipped his head and whispered a hot breath across her bare shoulder before his mouth caressed the skin below her ear. "Body heat."

She choked on a moan. All the reasons why she didn't want this, want him, fled her brain whenever he got this close. They might be in cold water, but a fire had started in her core, and little flames licked at her wherever his hands touched.

His fingers at her hips played with the lace of her blue boyshorts. "I like these. Practical but sexy." He leaned back, and she missed the warmth of his chest pressed against hers. "Do you always wear matching underwear?"

Desire stirred in the depths of his gaze, but something else, some emotion she couldn't quite pin down, held her transfixed. "Not always."

A slow smile started across his lips, as if he thought she'd worn them for him. She hadn't . . .

had she?

The hands at her hips started to trail up her stomach, and her brain did its mush thing. What were they talking about?

His thumb brushed the side of her bra, and a different kind of shiver shook her. Her eyes slitted with pleasure, and her gaze slid to his mouth.

Underwear! Her brain stirred enough to scream the word at her in an attempt to pull her from Blaze's thrall.

They *were* talking about underwear. "Do you always wear boxers?"

A grin flashed his white teeth at her in an expression she could only describe as devilish. "Oh, not always."

Her stomach fluttered in response, and she bit her lip.

Too damn sexy.

A distant bell of warning pealed in her head, but no part of her cared to listen to it.

Blaze dipped his mouth to her other shoulder and rasped in her ear, "What do you say we warm up in the grass over there?"

Yes! Please!

Her body had taken control, leaving no room to think about consequences. "Ye—"

As soon as she started to form the word, Blaze

gripped the underside of her thighs and walked backward until he pulled them both from the cold water. She wrapped her arms around his neck. They'd only gone a step when his hands left her thighs, and she nearly lost her grip. The water lapped at her feet, trying to pull them down.

His fingers feathered over her left side as he said, "Does that hurt?" All hints of seduction had gone from his tone.

Braylin glanced down at her rib cage and shrugged at the red bruises stretching a few inches across her skin. The cold water had dulled the ache enough that she barely noticed it. "Not really."

He said nothing in response, but his jaw clenched, the muscle bulging as he ground his teeth.

"Blaze?"

He stared past her shoulder, and when her legs started to slip, he did nothing to catch them as she slid off his body.

A cold front swooped in and smothered all the heat they'd created together. She wrapped her arms around herself and shivered.

When Blaze stomped across the pebbles and out of the water, Braylin followed.

Why is he so upset?

He stopped in the grass, gripping the back of his head with both hands.

After all the fighting they'd done, she'd never seen him angry. Unease skittered across her shoulders in a shadowy caress. Her voice didn't come out as strong as she wanted it to when she dared to ask, "Hey, what's wrong?"

He still wouldn't look at her. When he spoke, it was a low growl. "You should've let me look at that."

She reached for his arm as she tried to soothe him. "Really, I'm fine."

"You don't know that!" He whirled and exploded on her.

She stumbled back a step at his ferocity.

"I've been pushing you to climb all damn day, and you could have—" He cut himself off with a shake of the head. His mouth looked grim when he opened it again. "What if it's not just your skin that's bruised? Or worse, what if you cracked a rib, Braylin?"

She watched his chest shake with his breaths as she tried to understand why he was so upset. They'd been in a helicopter crash. Of course, they were a little banged up, but she'd know if her rib injury was more serious than just some tenderness.

Keeping her voice even, she tried to reason with him. "Look, my muscles are tired from climbing, and my ribs are a little sore, but that's all." She lifted a hand to his too-tight jaw. Her palm scraped against stubble as she soothed, "I'd be in a lot more pain if I'd cracked them. I'm okay. I promise."

The seconds stretched as she pleaded with her eyes for him to calm down. Each one added a knot to the rope around her insides. Eventually, his jaw relaxed, and she let out a breath she hadn't realized she'd been holding.

His eyes were unreadable when he spoke. "It'll be getting dark soon. We should find somewhere to make camp."

CHAPTER 12

Truths Shine in the Dark

"Dammit!" Blaze growled when he knocked the back of his head again on the same jagged piece of rock.

After they left the lake, they'd found an abandoned mine to use as shelter for the night. He'd first noticed the old, rusted rail the miners had used to move carts in and out. The rails had ended at the bottom of a crag, and when he'd gotten a closer look, he'd spotted the boarded-up entrance.

They'd pulled the boards off to make an entryway, earning him a splinter in the process. Once he'd made sure the walls were secure enough, they'd moved in. He figured it would at least keep them from being exposed to any other wild animals.

Braylin had been surprised, but finding an abandoned mine wasn't uncommon in Colorado. Over 20,000 deserted silver and gold mine sites littered the state.

Unfortunately, the shaft in this one had caved in, starting less than ten feet from the entrance, which left them an overhang around six feet in height and barely four in width. Even sitting, it was . . . cozy. And dark as hell. Not that he minded, but it meant he couldn't see the rocky walls, and somehow, his head connected with a sharp point—twice.

It didn't help his mood, which hadn't improved since he'd seen the bruises on Braylin's side. He couldn't stop berating himself for not checking her out sooner. She could've been hurt worse than either of them realized, and that fact scared the shit out of him.

Broken ribs were serious. They could puncture organs or cause internal bleeding. With an injury like that and no way to get medical care . . . the prognosis wouldn't be good.

He couldn't seem to let that go. The possibility of losing her was a column of smoke slowly choking all the air from his lungs.

"Maybe we should've stayed at the lake." Her

voice startled him out of his thoughts.

Blaze tried to sigh out some of the tension making his skin buzz. "No, it's fine. The bugs would've been unbearable without a campfire." With this area still under a drought, he hadn't wanted to risk it. One stray ember floating into the tall grasses by the lake could've sparked another wildfire, and they didn't need anything else to run from.

"Do you mind if I . . ." In the pitch-black darkness, his ears pricked at the sound of her scooting across the dirt floor of the mine, then her hand connected with his left shoulder. She snatched it away almost immediately. "Sorry, I didn't want to bump you, but I was sitting on the rail."

"You don't have to apologize for touching me." The comment came out harsher than he'd intended, and Blaze took a deep breath, ready to apologize.

She beat him to it. Her voice was hesitant and quieter than he'd ever heard her speak. "I know. I just didn't want to hit your wounded shoulder."

He'd put it back in the sling but barely noticed the injury. The only pain he could focus on was hers and whatever she might be feeling based on the color he'd seen across her ribcage.

"My arm is fine." Damn, that came out rougher than he meant, too. He cleared his throat. "You bumped the other one anyway. How are your ribs?"

"Probably colorful, not that I can see them. But they don't hurt. At least if I don't touch them."

"It doesn't hurt when you breathe?"

"No, not really."

Damned if that didn't spike his blood pressure. Unclenching his jaw, he asked as mildly as he could manage, "'No' or 'Not really?' There's a difference, Braylin."

"No."

He wasn't sure he believed her. "You'd tell me if it did, right?" This time, his tone was practically a plea.

"Of course." The response came too fast to be believable. "It's kind of cold in here. And I—" A sneeze loud enough to reverberate in their tiny space and echo off the walls cut off her words. "Whoa, that was intense. All the stale air and dust is tickling my nose."

"Yeah, there's probably mold in here too." Maybe spending the night in the mine had been a bad idea. "Did that hurt your ribs?"

"It doesn't smell moldy."

Ever reasonable. But he needed to know the

answer to his other question. He cautioned himself not to bark it at her as he asked again. "Did it hurt, Braylin?"

"No, it didn't hurt to sneeze." The patient understanding in her voice eased his mind—a little.

"Good." He cleared his throat and inhaled. No hints of mold, but it smelled like dirt, damp, and—*fuck me*—lavender and vanilla. Her perfume made him think of the kiss they'd shared at the lake.

Remembering what they'd almost done made his pants grow too tight. He'd acted like an idiot. They could've made love in a gorgeous location, but he'd let that opportunity slip through his fingers instead. And it wasn't like he could pick up where they'd left off in this dark-ass mine. He wanted to take his time and explore her body, watching her react to every single touch. If he couldn't see her . . . there was zero chance of that happening.

"Are you comfortable?"

The question made him bark out a harsh laugh. "Not even a little bit." Between the cold, packed dirt floor, the uneven rock walls, and the hard-on stretching his zipper, Blaze wasn't even in the same realm as comfortable.

Her laugh in response felt forced, but she said, "Me neither. Can we . . . do you want to, um . . ."

If he could see her, he'd bet she chewed on her lip, and for the first time in hours, Blaze felt a smile tug at the corner of his mouth when he understood what she was trying to get out. He would be more than happy to cuddle with her.

"Yes, come here." Reaching with his left hand, he searched for her leg in the darkness.

"Oh, that's my—"

He cut off what she no doubt thought would be a helpful suggestion. "I know."

One of her hands landed on top of his. "Could you—"

He pushed further off the wall. "Just let me mov—"

"Yes, but . . . ." The air in front of his face moved, and he knew he'd almost gotten slapped. She seemed oblivious to that fact.

As they talked over one another, they started a catfight, accidentally swatting each other until they'd become a tangle of arms and legs. It was frustrating as hell but also comical as fuck.

Blaze was about to tell Braylin to just sit still when she started laughing—loudly. Though hysteria tinged the sound, it curved his lips. The parts of her entwined with him shook, and as he felt her laugh, the ball of emotions he'd been battling all afternoon deflated. He tried to find her face in the dark while his chest quivered, joining her in hysterical laughter.

"Oh my God!" Braylin gasped between riotous chuckling. Her laughter muffled her next words, and he only understood some of them. "Idiot" and "flashlight" caught his attention right before their little haven lit up with the beam from her cellphone.

He grinned at the beautiful face covered in mirth staring back at him. "Hi."

"Hi." She snort-laughed, making him chuckle.

"Should we try that again?" His gaze fell to her lips, still curved in humor. *Or we could make out instead.*

"I think so."

This time, they moved together in perfect harmony. She settled into his good side, and he wrapped his arm around her. When her leg snaked over the top of his, he nearly jerked away, but she managed to avoid the evidence of how much more he wanted to do with her than cuddling. He hoped the light from her phone didn't give him away.

"Maybe we should cut it off now, conserve the battery." Because that's why he wanted the damned thing turned off.

"Good idea." She picked up the cellphone and plunged them back into darkness.

A minute passed in comfortable silence before she whispered, "This is nice."

"Yeah." It *was* nice. He wanted to tell her how perfect she felt in his arms, but as soon as he opened his mouth, he quickly closed it. Would she even believe him?

"Can I ask you something?"

Her head lay on his chest, and he played with the ends of her ponytail. "Anything, angel."

"How'd you get the name, 'Blaze'?"

His lips twisted into a self-deprecating smile. "As a rookie, I had an unfortunate incident with my drip torch."

The torch consisted of a metal canister holding fuel with a handle attached to the side. When not in use, the igniter stowed away within the canister. It was one of several tools wildland firefighters used that allowed them to fight fire with fire by burning away fuels like grass and brush before they had a chance to feed a wildfire. A drip torch wasn't half as cool as the PyroShot, though. He'd never gotten the chance to play with that fire launcher or the ignition spheres it shot out at a high rate of speed. Now, he doubted he ever would.

She scoffed and lifted her head even though it was too dark to see into his face. "Oh, come on! You *have* to tell me the whole story."

An idea sparked, and Blaze grinned, his voice teasing. "Only if you agree to make a trade."

He felt the skepticism in her tone. "What do you mean? What kind of trade?"

The half of his blood throbbing below his waist wanted to give her a very different answer, but he ignored it. "I tell you my embarrassing story and you tell me what made you so upset Friday night."

* * *

Braylin's whole body solidified with panic. How did he know she'd had a total meltdown after their rendezvous in the storage closet?

"You were clearly pissed about something at the hangar this morning too. If it's anything I can help with, I'd like to know." Blaze's voice cut through the alarms going off in her head.

Relief turned her muscles to jelly. He'd meant before they'd had sex at the bar, not . . . *after*. She could tell him that. No problem.

"Deal, but you first."

With her head on his chest, she felt the grumble before she heard it. "Fine. But try not to hold it against me."

A quip about having a low enough opinion about him already sprang to her lips, but she didn't voice it. The remark was a knee-jerk reaction—her armed response to protect the walls she'd built—but it wouldn't have been true. Instead, she only teased, "We'll see."

"I got the nickname five years ago when I was a rookie. I, uh . . ."

"Tell me you didn't light someone on fire with your torch."

"No! Geez, it wasn't that bad." His body shifted under her chin, and she made a noise of protest. "Sorry, there was a rock."

She grinned into the pitch-black emptiness. "Are you stalling?"

"No. But let me preface my story by saying this happens more often than you'd think."

"U-huh. Spill it, hotshot."

She thought he ran his hand down his face, but in the dark, she couldn't be sure. "A lot of us wear our drip torches secured to our backpacks. Well, mine had leaked fuel onto my pack, and when we started our prescribed burn operation . . . it caught on fire."

"Holy shit, were you still wearing it?"

"Yeah. I didn't even notice it. One of the guys

on my crew flagged me down, pointing at my back and screaming 'Blaze!', 'Blaze!'. He helped me shrug it off and extinguish it."

Her hand on his side unconsciously gripped his shirt in a fist. She couldn't imagine what she'd do in that situation. He had literally been on fire. "Were you burned?"

"No. Got lucky, I guess. But after that, everyone called me Blaze since I'd set myself ablaze with the damn torch. I got taken off firing operations after that." His voice ended on an acidic note, but she felt glad he wasn't working prescribed burns. His job was dangerous enough without adding fuel to the fire—literally.

His hand covered her fist, and her cheeks heated. She didn't like the idea of him being hurt. Loosening her grip, she told him, "I'm sorry that happened, but I'm glad you weren't hurt." She had another thought and voiced it. "Do you like the name? Because if it bugs you, I can call you Noah."

He didn't immediately respond, and the long, shrill call of a mountain cicada penetrated their shelter, filling the silence.

Did I misstep?

The insect's call ended, then another began. Finally, he spoke, "I've gotten used to being Blaze, but . . . there's more to it than that."

She wished she could see his face but knew she shouldn't waste her phone battery. Calling for help was the priority, especially since they'd seen no more search and rescue aircraft, and at some point in their trek, she might actually get a signal and be able to. "What do you mean?"

His diaphragm moved with his sigh. "That's not the only crap thing that happened to me my first year as a hotshot."

It was her turn to spill about her lying crew chief, but she couldn't help asking, "What else happened?"

His answer didn't come right away. After several tense seconds, she felt an expulsion of air on the top of her head that sounded like 'fuckit' before he said, "I went home after my roll and found my long-time girlfriend cheating on me." Bitterness crept into his tone. "Apparently, fourteen days was too long for her to wait for me."

"I'm sorry." Braylin squeezed his hand. "She didn't deserve you." *Oh, shit! Did I just say that aloud?*

Braylin's pulse sped, and heat flooded her body while she had a mini-freakout over whether he would brush her comment off or take it further. Half of her was petrified that he would, and the other half wanted him to because she'd spoken the truth. As much as she'd tried to hate him, Blaze wasn't all the things she'd thought. He hadn't been the one breaking hearts. He'd had his crushed instead.

Even though it broke her rule about seeing men she worked with, she'd been ready to give into Blaze's charm by the lake, but after he'd blown from hot to cold, she didn't know where they stood.

When he spoke, his voice sounded serious. Any trace of his cockiness had gone. "No, she didn't. I left and didn't go back to California for the rest of the season." His arm tightened around Braylin's middle and calmed the nerves her confession had caused. She relaxed into his side, settling into the scent of smoke that never seemed to leave him as he continued his story, "Being away, I got to be Blaze. I didn't have to be Noah, this rookie kid who messed up with his drip torch and got cheated on by his girlfriend. Instead, I became one of the crew, and I started to like that new me."

Braylin snorted to lighten the mood. "So, Blaze, the cocky hotshot, was born?"

She heard his smile when he answered, "Basically."

Chuckling, she snuggled closer. Blaze's fingers

wound around her hair, but she didn't want him to remove them. Lying with him like this felt . . . right. Like having something she'd been missing for too long. The rain after a long, *long* drought.

"So, now you know about my defense mechanism." His finger twirled her hair in a spiral. "What's the story behind yours?"

Every fiber in her being went taut. It might seem only fair to tell him about her ex after he'd told her about his, but—

I can't.

She wasn't ready to walk down that path yet. Instead, she shifted off Blaze, intent on making a bed on the ground and curling her arm under her head as a pillow. "We should sleep."

CHAPTER 13

I Spy with My Little Eye

The weather was no different from the day before, but somehow, it felt hotter. Sweat left a constant sheen on Blaze's face that he'd stopped bothering to wipe away. He and Braylin had been climbing for the last hour on nothing but water and fumes. They'd shared his power bar yesterday at the lake. It had been their last bit of food, and he knew Braylin had to be just as hungry as he was this morning. His stomach agreed because it growled loud enough to wake a hibernating bear, scaring the birds tweeting above their heads into silence.

Blaze glanced up at the canopy of green as each step became harder to take. Even his boots seemed heavier; they were extra weights attached to his feet, making his leg muscles scream in protest. He inhaled, and the air felt too thin to fill his lungs properly. While that sucked ass, it meant they had to be getting close to the mountain's peak.

Glancing behind him, he worried about how Braylin fared. He'd already stopped them twice to ask about her ribs and breathing. The second time was only ten minutes ago, and she'd nearly bitten his head off. Maybe he *was* being a tad overprotective, but . . . he cared about her. Telling her about Sloane had been confirmation enough of that.

A frown tugged at his lips. He'd divulged his past, but she'd clammed up as soon as he'd asked about hers. He kicked at a rock in his path as disappointment tightened his chest. What did he have to do to get Braylin to trust him enough to open up?

At least after she'd shut down about her past, he'd gotten her to explain what had upset her on Friday night. He'd been surprised to hear about her crew chief. He'd liked Roger as soon as he'd met the man, especially seeing how he'd acted around Braylin. Roger had been big brother protective of her the moment Blaze showed up. But despite how much the man might care for her, he'd clearly made some bad choices.

A gambling addiction was one thing, but if Roger had gotten in over his head bad enough to steal from Leif Aero . . .

What lengths would the people Roger owed go to when he didn't pay up?

The thought made Blaze's mouth dry out with worry. He hoped like hell Braylin hadn't gotten herself caught in the middle.

"Blaze! Look!"

His head snapped toward her at the shout.

"No, there!"

When she pulled up beside him, he followed her pointing finger past the pine and spruce trees in their path. Through the timber, he glimpsed stone and—

"It's a structure! What do you think it is?"

The only thing that made sense at this altitude would be . . . "A lookout tower."

"Hurry! Do you think it's still manned?" She outpaced him in her excitement, and he didn't have the heart to burst her bubble.

The only lookouts in the state still employing fire scouts were located in national parks. This one had likely been abandoned for a long time, but maybe there'd be something useful left behind.

As they drew closer, the trees thinned until

they disappeared altogether. When they broke from the forest, the tower became easier to see. Not a hundred yards away, it stood forlorn at the tip of the peak. The path up to its door consisted of faded dirt, loose gravel, and broken rocks. Nothing green, not even a weed, dared grow among the desolate ground.

Braylin had stopped at the tree line with him. The obvious run-down state of the structure likely dashed her hopes. The stone foundation crumbled away in one corner as if some mountain giant had taken a bite out of it. Above the stone first floor, a wooden deck appeared. Weathered and rickety, it wrapped around the second level. Beyond the deck stood a room that was all windows with a hipped roof looking ready to collapse. The metal shingles covering it had been torn away in sections.

Blaze nudged Braylin with his elbow. "Hey, maybe there'll be a radio."

She nodded and seemed to shake off the disappointment. "Or non-perishables. Right now, I'm not sure I'd even care if they were expired."

Blaze chuckled but couldn't help agreeing. "Yeah, me either."

The inside of the lookout proved to be in better shape than the exterior suggested. Though it was no longer in use, the tower had been shut up tightly. The hinges on the weathered wooden door squeaked when Blaze pushed it open.

Light came in through a small, square window to the right of the door, showcasing a healthy layer of dust on the furniture inside, but no stray debris littered the concrete floor of the twelve-by-twelve lower room. A narrow metal desk lined the wall adjacent to the door, and a cot mirrored its position on the opposite wall.

"Honey, I'm home!" The remark earned him a snort and a swat from Braylin, but he just grinned and stepped inside.

"Well, I'd expected worse." Her voice interrupted his examination of the items piled on top of the desk. File folders, binoculars, and office supplies formed a minor mountain as if everything had been placed there in preparation for packing, which had never occurred.

Catching her eye, he nodded. "I did, too." He gestured her over with a head tilt. "I think there's probably a base station buried under here."

Her eyes widened before she hurried to his side. "Could we get so lucky?"

"I feel pretty damn lucky whenever you're around, Braylin." The words flew out of his mouth without a thought, and they both stilled as what he'd said sank in.

Their eyes met and held. He expected her to scoff and retort with a quip, but she gave his hand a quick squeeze and merely said, "Thank you," in a soft voice before turning away.

Promising.

The fact she hadn't turned his comment into a joke warmed Blaze's chest, feeding the fire of hope still burning there. Carelessly, he shoved aside a faded white coffee mug and dust-covered binders until he found what he'd been looking for.

Glancing over his shoulder, he asked, "Do you want the good news or the bad news?"

Braylin dropped the blanket she'd been shaking out and moved to his side. "A radio?"

"Yep, that's the good news." He pushed buttons and twisted knobs on the old analog machine with no response. "The bad news is it's dead."

"Okay, well, not great, but maybe there's a generator?" She didn't sound half as deflated as he'd expected. "Let's check upstairs."

The two levels only connected on the exterior, so he followed Braylin back outside. By the eastern corner, wooden stairs led up to the observation deck. At first glance, he wasn't sure they'd hold.

From behind Braylin, he warned, "Be careful. Test the step before you put any weight on it."

She tossed him an exasperated expression over her shoulder. "Do I look like an idiot?"

Forgot who I was talking to.

Not at all perturbed by her question, Blaze gave her his best earnest face. "My apologies, ma'am." He tipped a fake hat in her direction. "Lead the way."

She shook her head and turned back toward the stairs, but not before he caught the smile she'd tried to hide. It made him remember the last time she'd smiled like that—the kiss they'd shared after the moose. He wondered what he'd have to do to make her eyes turn gold again.

A kiss had worked before, so . . . If they found a way to generate electricity with solar power, it would likely take some time, which might be a good opportunity to make use of the cot downstairs.

Blaze blinked against the sunshine, and a wide grin spread across his face at the thought. The added bonus of the sight of Braylin's tight ass right in front of him only stretched it wider. She really was blessed in that department.

Maybe she does hella squats when she works out.

"Damn. That's a long climb down." She'd stopped at the top of the stairs, and Blaze couldn't help but take advantage of the opening she'd left him.

Reaching the step behind her, he caged her in, capturing her with his good arm and molding her body into his to peek over her shoulder. Below their vantage point, the peak sloped down into smaller hills before leveling out in a valley of brush hundreds of feet below.

A path snaked through it, and he pointed it out to her. "But look, the road to civilization."

"You know what I don't see?" The question was rhetorical because she didn't wait for him to answer. "A cell tower." With a sigh, she pulled out her phone and powered it on, but no little bars appeared on the screen.

"Figures." She put her phone away and leaned back. "If we weren't stuck out here, this would be really pretty."

When her amazing ass brushed against him, Blaze's stomach muscles contracted. Swallowing down his desire, he told her, "Stuck or not, it's a gorgeous view."

Their vantage point had to be the highest for what seemed like miles. As far as his eyes could see, mountains covered in green trees and yellow wildflowers stretched to the horizon below a sky painted a vibrant blue hue. But the thing he enjoyed most about it was gazing across that landscape with Braylin in his arms. The moments bled into one another while they took it all in.

Too soon, she pulled out of his embrace. "We should see what's up here."

"Yeah." Before he dragged her back down to that cot. Blaze watched her hips sway as she walked away. When she disappeared around the corner of the L-shaped deck, he adjusted himself and followed.

A distant column of smoke stopped Blaze on the side of the deck facing the forest. The fire they'd started still burned. Out of habit, he pulled out his weather meter. What little wind it registered wouldn't do much to spread the flames, but he couldn't shake the uneasy feeling in the pit of his stomach. He didn't like being cut off from his crewmates. Pocketing the tool, he turned away in search of Braylin.

A windowed door stood open behind him, leading into the interior of the top room. A quick glance around told him up here hadn't fared as well as downstairs. The rain had clearly gotten in from the stains on the wooden rafters and the tell-tale smell of rot. The walls seemed sturdy enough, but he didn't feel as comfortable with the roof.

"Let's be quick. I don't trust this thing not to collapse on us."

Braylin rummaged through the mass of nature debris covering the center table. Dead leaves and pine needles littered the floor around her. When he drew closer, he saw she'd uncovered an alidade. The device consisted of a topographic map with two sights for getting the bearings of a fire.

She glanced up at his approach. "At least now we know where we are."

"That'll come in handy if we can get the radio to work."

Braylin grinned at him. "We can."

He couldn't help a responding grin. "What else have you found, Nancy Drew?"

She motioned toward a metal cabinet standing in the far corner. Leaning next to it were solar panels. If the tower had used solar energy, then the batteries they powered were around here somewhere. Blaze moved to the cabinet and opened it up.

Paydirt.

He forgot all about batteries as his eyes fell on the canned goods stored in the cabinet. The offerings consisted of potted meat, SPAM, corn, and green beans. They could do worse.

A crash sounded behind him, followed by Braylin's curse. "You're not you when you're hungry, babe. Eat a Snickers." He tossed the remark over his shoulder and saw her rubbing a shin.

"Don't tease me like that." She straightened with a whine, "I'd sell my body for a Snickers right now."

He turned, then leaned against the cabinet and crossed his arms. "Well, that makes things interesting. What would you do for some SPAM and a can of creamed corn?"

Her pretty hazel eyes narrowed. "Is that what's in the cabinet?"

He smirked. "You didn't answer my question."

She advanced, raising her chin to scowl at him in defiance. "Move out of the way, hotshot."

He clucked his tongue at her. "As soon as you answer the question, *angel.*"

Without warning, her expression changed from frustrated Amazon to sultry courtesan. Her lashes lowered in a coy gesture before she murmured, "That's probably worth a blow job."

Her words sank in, and Blaze's heartbeat stuttered. When her finger traced his zipper, he blinked stupidly and forgot how to speak.

Whatever game she was playing, he was up for it.

Then her hand cupped him through his pants; his eyes closed and he swallowed a groan. Her touch lit him up like throwing gasoline on a fire. His pulse took off, and he forgot all about food. The only thing he wanted to eat was her.

Blaze was picturing her spread-eagled on the cot downstairs when he felt a poke in his groin. Opening his eyes, he found Braylin grinning at him, the point of her knife dangerously close to his junk. His eyes only widened a *little* bit. "You wouldn't."

"I don't know, Blaze. I get hangry, and you're standing between me and food so . . ." Her grin turned sharp. "Are you willing to try me?"

Maybe he was a masochist because his dick twitched at her threat.

She glanced down at the weapon with a sigh. "It really would be a shame."

Blaze's throat had gone dry, and he swallowed to clear it. He didn't think she'd actually stick him with that knife of hers, but sexual fantasies aside, he didn't care to test that theory either. "I know when to cut my losses." Stepping out of her way, he added, "All yours, sweet thing."

CHAPTER 14

Nectar of the Gods

SPAM was Braylin's new favorite form of meat. She didn't even care that it was cold or that visible fat had congealed around the block of pink pork. It was the best thing she'd ever tasted, so much so that she couldn't help the moans emitting from her throat with each bite she took.

"Do you plan on sharing any of that ambrosia?"

She opened her eyes to find Blaze staring at her with a raised brow. Her hunger had taken over, and she'd gone a bit animal once he'd moved away from the cabinet. She may or may not still be guarding it from her perch on top.

Watching him, where he leaned a little too casually against the mapping table, she sliced another chunk off the canned meat and lifted it to her lips. With her tongue, she shoveled it into her mouth and chewed. The squishiness didn't bother her, nor did its intense saltiness. To her, it tasted like the nectar of the gods. But she'd eaten enough to think clearly and realized Blaze probably deserved some, too.

Once she'd swallowed, she smiled at him and offered the remainder of the can. "You said something about cream corn?"

"Yeah," he smirked and angled his head toward the cabinet. "In the trove you're guarding."

Braylin hopped down and opened the door. Once she'd located the can, she wasted no time opening it. A couple of quick punctures using the tip of her knife, and she'd created a hole big enough for the corn to flow through.

If the SPAM was ambrosia, the creamed corn was manna from heaven. Sweet and gooey, it stuck to her tongue like the best chocolate dessert, and she moaned even louder.

"Fuck, Braylin." Blaze's growl stopped her feasting.

She licked some of the goodness off her lip and met his stare. "What?"

"If you keep making those noises, I'm going to

. . ." he trailed off and looked away, swallowing hard.

She set the can of corn aside and closed the distance between them. "You're going to what?"

His pupils had dilated to the point very little blue remained in his gaze when his head snapped down to hers. "I want to make love to you—slowly. But those moans . . ." His hands lifted as though to pull her close, but they fell back to his sides, balled into fists. "All I can think about right now is fucking you against one of these windows."

A shiver of pleasure at his words nearly had her moaning again. Knowing she had that effect on him was exactly what she needed, but as appealing as his warning sounded, she had a better idea.

"Mmm," humming in her throat, she invaded his space, standing on her toes to whisper in his ear, "Maybe we should use that cot downstairs instead."

* * *

The dark blanket she'd shaken out went down against the army-green canvas of the cot. It was really only wide enough for one of them, but Braylin had a plan for how they could get around that.

Before she could ask Blaze to sit, he demanded, "Lie down."

Braylin knew how to follow orders, but she preferred giving them.

When she opened her mouth to protest, he placed a finger to her lips with a smile. "I know you don't like being told what to do." His head tilted, his mouth skimming along her cheek on the way to her ear. "But I'll make it worth your while."

His breath moving over her skin sent a fiery shiver down her back. Still, she arched a brow at him. "We'll see about that."

His soft chuckle made her stomach flutter, but he stopped her with a hand on her collarbone before she could do as he'd demanded. "Wait."

His head lowered, his tongue tracing that line of bone, and then she felt his hands at her shirt buttons. Flares of sensation followed the trail of his tongue, making the air back up in her lungs. When she spoke, her voice came out breathy. "I can do that."

She lifted her hands to undress herself, but Blaze captured them and hooked her palms behind her back. "You know what you can do for me, Braylin?"

"Hmm?" Why was he still talking when all she wanted to do was *feel*?

"Let go."

She blinked in confusion at his patient stare. "Let go of what?"

He released her hands, and she acquiesced, letting him remove her shirt. Even though she couldn't help thinking she would've done it faster.

Maybe he doesn't want fast?

His gaze fell to her injury, and she glanced down at her ribcage. The red had turned into colorful blue and purple bruising, but it no longer pained her.

Afraid he would stop again at the sight, she opened her mouth—to say what she wasn't sure—but he spoke instead. "So strong." His fingers caressed her bruised skin, then traveled north, just teasing the sides of her breasts. She shuddered at the contact. "You amaze me, Braylin."

Her eyes widened; she had no idea how to respond. Thankfully, he didn't need one. His head dipped again, and he kissed each bruise with such care and gentleness that she started to soften. Blaze had the ability to dull her edges until she became as malleable as a marshmallow.

Mayday, mayday!

She ignored the warning screaming in her head and closed her eyes as his hands—those giant, calloused hands—fondled her breasts through the blue lace of her bra. His thumbs brushed across her nipples, and her brain went fuzzy.

"Let me be in control. Just this once." His voice was a low rasp before he slid the straps of her bra off with his teeth. They scraped against her skin, lighting spot fires along their path. "And if you don't like it. It's your way from there on out."

She already loved what he was doing with his hands and mouth, but could she submit to him like this? Could she . . . trust him?

His gaze tracked hers before he lowered his head for a kiss. Her arms wrapped around his neck in reflex, pulling him closer, craving his hardness against her as his mouth urged her to surrender. The salty flavor of the meat on his tongue mixed with the sweet corn on hers, and she couldn't resist the combination. When it came to Blaze's lips on hers, she had no power. Her entire body liquified and melted against him.

In this, at least, I'll try. Because she cared enough to try to give him what he wanted.

Floating on a river of lazy warmth, she broke the kiss to tell him, "All right."

His smile was slow, lighting his entire face as

it spread. "Good girl."

Normally, she would've complained about that comment, but Blaze's hands had slipped inside the flight suit tied around her waist. His lips lowered to hers again, then a finger grazed the outside of her underwear, and her breath stuttered to a halt. When that finger dipped inside, she moaned into his mouth.

He continued to stroke her, and she clamped onto his shoulders as her legs threatened to drop her.

Mmm. Keep doing that.

But he didn't. His hands moved to her waist, and his forehead dropped to hers. "You're so wet."

Braylin had to bite her tongue to keep from telling him not to stop. She'd agreed to let him lead. But it didn't mean she couldn't snap her displeasure. "That's kind of the point, hotshot."

His answering grin was an ignition sphere launched at her ovaries; they caught fire on impact. "You didn't think it'd be that easy, did you, angel? I won't be finished with you until you're putty in my hands."

Holding her gaze, he knelt in front of her and tugged her underwear and flight suit to the floor. His hands and then his mouth started new brush fires as they trailed down her legs to help her step out of the clothing. When she was bare but for her shoes, he stood.

"Lie down, Braylin."

The fire in her body was too hot for her brain to handle. It drugged her like a fever, her thoughts and movements slower than they should be. "But my boots. . ."

"We'll get to those." His hand cruised down her stomach as he dropped his head to her ear. "Lie down."

She shuddered at the feel of his breath moving across her neck while his fingers teased her entrance, but she nodded, willing to do as he'd asked. The metal legs of the cot ground against the cement floor as she climbed on top of it.

"I want you to touch yourself."

Her eyes had half closed, reveling in the sensation of his fingers tracing idle circles against her thighs, but at his comment, they widened. "Touch . . . myself?"

"Mm-hmm." His tongue licked the back of her knee, and then his dark eyes pierced hers. "Show me what you like, Braylin."

She wasn't a blusher, but his demand made the entirety of her skin combust. She stiffened, raising up on her elbows with a flaming face. "I can't."

He cocked an eyebrow at her. "Are you going to tell me you've never pleasured yourself?"

Her hackles instantly rose. "No! But—"

Triumph laced his grin. "Then show me."

Could she?

She'd never touched herself in front of a partner before, and she wasn't sure how she felt about it other than embarrassed. Her cheeks heated like a sunburn. Except, there was something utterly erotic about his request.

Still, she glared at him. The man always had to challenge her. It was infuriating but—

He'd been blessed with magical hands. They were doing things to her thighs that made her fall back onto the cot.

Maybe if she closed her eyes . . .

Taking a deep breath, Braylin trailed a finger across her chest and down the valley of her breasts until she reached her center. Though her breath hitched with nerves and excitement, she applied pressure and then parted her folds, sliding her finger through the wetness there.

Knowing he watched her heightened the pleasure flooding her body. A powerful pull drew all the heat to her core, soaking her as she let go of her inhibitions. She circled the swollen bundle of nerves at the apex of her thighs, then added a second finger before dipping inside her damp heat.

"Fuck, that's hot." Blaze had been removing her boots, but he'd stopped when she dared to open her eyes. The remaining one stayed clasped in his grip while his gaze glued to her moving hand.

She bit her lip as she worked her palm over her most sensitive spot. The pressure that meant her release was close built in her core. She fisted her other hand in the blanket, and her eyes closed again.

"Stop!"

Braylin froze, blinking at his abrupt tone.

He dropped her boot to the floor with a thud, then grasped her thighs and pulled her to the edge of the cot. His head lowered to her sex, and he growled, "You're not coming until I get a taste."

She'd thought she'd been hot from embarrassment before, but the look he gave her unleashed a firestorm in her blood.

He licked up her slit, adding to the pressure in her core, threatening to tear her to shreds. "Oh God."

This time, she was the goddess and he the worshiping supplicant. She burned from the inside out as he worked her with his tongue, his teeth, and his hands until no part of her had been left untouched by the blaze.

Her body writhed, and she whimpered, the sound unfamiliar to her ears. She was losing herself but couldn't seem to care. Her hips bucked, begging for more, and he answered.

"Scream for me, Braylin. I want to see you lose control."

She was too far gone to wonder over his obsession with control. The only thing that existed now was the wildfire raging underneath her skin. The flames from it increased the pressure holding the cap on her release until it became unbearable, ripping free with a scream from her throat. Her hands fisted in the blanket. Then she flew apart.

The orgasm tore through her body in an explosion of heat, scattering bits and pieces of her to the wind. Her head ended up in the clouds, floating in a serene and cooling calm across the bright sky.

"God, you're beautiful."

She wasn't sure if the voice sounded inside her head or out. Slowly, ripples of sensation penetrated as her body pieced itself back together. She opened her eyes to see Blaze kissing her thigh.

When his gaze met hers, she sighed. *There* was

the sky she'd floated in. Those dreamy blue eyes that she loved. She lifted a finger to his cheek, and her arm muscles protested, still languishing in the soft afterglow of what he'd done to her. "Thank you," she murmured with a smile.

* * *

Her eyes had turned that elusive gold again, making him wonder if the color came from her release or something more.

He kissed his way up her body, pausing to stare down at the sleepy smile on her face. Watching Braylin surrender had nearly made him bust through his zipper, but now, seeing her so relaxed filled him with an overpowering sense of pride. He'd done that for her—given her peace.

He'd wanted to show her what she could have if she let someone else take the reins, but the primal part of him knew that *someone* would only ever be him. Because she was his.

Even if she doesn't know it yet.

He unbuttoned his shirt, watching her as he undressed. Her breasts shifted with each inhale, and her hands lifted, touching herself there without prompting. Her hands on her chest only reminded him how she'd looked with them between her legs. The image had been burned into his memory; he felt ready to blow just thinking about what she'd done for him. And her taste . . .

His blood throbbed in his ears as he hurried, fumbling with the buckle on his pants until he'd managed to nearly rip them open in his haste to be inside her. She'd been as sweet as the last drop of water for a man dying of thirst. He'd drunk in her juices and never wanted to stop.

Mine. All mine.

He kicked off his boots and checked himself as he nearly toppled over. He'd promised slow so he would build her up again and watch her fall apart.

A smirk crossed his lips, and he lowered his head to nip at her skin. When she gasped, he laved the mark with his tongue. "You're going to fly again, angel."

He could tell she was waking up because that smart mouth twisted, ready to flay him for biting her, no doubt. But he didn't let her speak, instead capturing that feisty tongue with his own.

Her sweet vanilla and floral scent flooded his senses, tightening the muscles below his belt, but he kept his hands gentle as they roamed over her, mindful of the bruising on her ribs. As she'd done every time before, she melted with his kiss.

With her body pliant beneath his, Blaze slipped inside her, swallowing the sweet little moan she made in the back of her throat.

Tight, warm . . . Fuck, she feels good.

But she was still so tight that he stopped to wait for her to adjust. Sweat broke out along his hairline, and he clenched his jaw against the desire to pump into her.

A groan shook his chest, and Braylin broke their kiss. "Are you okay? Is it your shoulder?"

He opened his eyes and would've laughed at the worried expression on her face if his body wasn't screaming at him in exquisite torture that had nothing to do with the pain in his shoulder. "No. My shoulder's fine," he managed to grind out.

To distract himself, he lowered his mouth to her breast, using his palm to cup the other one. Braylin wasn't overly big in that department, but she had just enough to fit into his mouth.

He licked and tasted, feasting on her until she squirmed beneath him. Her body arched into his when he nibbled on her, and he nearly lost the tether on his control. The position drove him in further, and he cursed, unable to keep from moving. He forced himself to slide in and out slowly, drawing out and building the pleasure for them both.

"Faster." She wrapped her legs around his

waist with the demand, lifting her hips to push him deeper.

"No." His response was a clipped growl as he put all his focus into keeping his strokes slow and steady.

When she opened her mouth to argue, he brought a hand between them while he thrust, to touch her the same way she'd shown him.

Her head fell back to the cot, her eyes closing. Soon, her breathing became as rapid as his, their bodies meeting and throwing sparks. With a groan, her hips urged him on, and he knew it was time for both of them to let go.

"Come with me, Braylin." At his strangled plea, her eyes opened, the hazel swirling with hazy pleasure. Her chocolate hair splayed around her head in a dark halo.

My angel.

He captured the image with his mind and stored it for later. When her gaze locked on his, she nodded. Blaze increased his speed, and she matched his new pace. The flames of the fire they created together grew higher and higher.

Their breaths mingled in frantic panting that drowned out the squeaking of the cot as they climbed their way to the peak. When he felt her convulse around him, his body tightened, a shudder working through him as they jumped off the ledge together.

CHAPTER 15

Catching Feelings

Fuck. Shit. Damn.

Braylin was in trouble. Like feet-sinking-fast-in-quicksand kind of trouble. Blaze was supposed to be off-limits because they worked together. Now she'd gone and . . . dared she say it?

Caught feelings.

She clenched her eyes tightly shut as her stomach roiled, and it wasn't from the expired canned goods she'd eaten. Their bodies remained flush on the cot, their hearts settled down from the same thundering rhythm they'd raced to, but her brain was too preoccupied to notice.

Maybe she just thought she was falling for him because of how good the sex had been.

Like an eleven *on a scale of one to five.*

Just thinking of everything they'd shared suffused her body with embarrassment *and* arousal. It had never been that intense before. *Never*. What the hell had Blaze done to her?

Clearly, her brain cells had been incinerated along with the rest of her.

Did I scream?

When he'd made her come again, she was pretty sure she'd been just as loud as the first time. If they weren't in the middle of nowhere, she'd probably be humiliated by that.

A frown tugged at her lips. So what if the man was a sex god? It didn't mean she wanted anything more from him than that . . . *Right?*

Regardless of what her brain tried to tell her, Braylin's body didn't seem to be listening. Her chest tightened uncomfortably, and she couldn't breathe. Opening her eyes, she found out why. The ends of Blaze's blonde hair tickled her cheek while his shoulder crushed her air supply. How long had they been lying like this? Time had ceased to exist after he'd made her explode into fireworks.

"Blaze," she gasped out. She would've pushed him off but didn't want to aggravate his injured shoulder accidentally.

He stirred with an unintelligible grunt. But at

least he lifted onto a forearm, allowing her to suck in some much-needed air. He blinked a few times. Then his eyes focused on her, and his mouth curved into a slow, satisfied smile. "Angel."

Don't smile. Don't smile. It would send the wrong message. *Dammit!* She sighed internally as her lips involuntarily answered his. *Why does he have to be so damn charming?*

"Um." Braylin chewed on her lip. What the hell should she say? "We should probably set up those solar panels."

Really, Braylin? Way to set some boundaries . . . that was a major facepalm moment. Her stomach twisted with anxiety while she waited for him to respond.

His smile didn't waver, but his eyes seemed clearer as he said, "We'll get to that." Then he shifted until he hovered directly over her. "But since I have you here . . ." His smile faded, his eyes becoming the soft blue that tempted her to drown her worries in it. "Tell me why you got out of the military."

Despite the heat of his body on hers, Braylin instantly went cold. Instinctively, her palms went up to push against his chest and free herself, but he cuffed them with one of his, trapping her hands between their bodies.

"Blaze," she warned through gritted teeth.

He ignored the glare she gave him, lowering his head to give tiny kisses across her neck until he reached her ear. "Won't you trust me, Braylin?"

Though her skin hummed where his mouth touched, a cold, empty pit still widened like a crevasse inside her. She shut her eyes while she debated with herself so she didn't have to stare into the emotions she didn't want to acknowledge in his. She'd wanted to set boundaries, to explain that this was only sex and it *had* to stay between them—period. If she were going to make him understand, it made sense to explain why, but opening that old wound . . .

A small gasp slipped from her lips when Blaze gently kissed each closed lid. Her eyes fluttered open, and she got caught in his hopeful stare. With a sigh as weighty as her resignation, Braylin decided to tell him about Rob. "I have rules."

Blaze lifted an eyebrow as if waiting to hear her demands.

She shook her head as best she could while lying underneath him on the cot. "No, I mean, I made rules for myself because of . . . what happened."

The blue of his eyes softened. "What happened?"

Braylin opened her mouth, and her throat closed as if it also refused to talk about this. Frustrated with herself, she shut her eyes and then swallowed hard before pushing out, "My ex-boyfriend ruined my career. We were in the same unit, and he . . ." *Fuck!* She didn't want to talk about this. Bile rose up her throat, but she forced it down. "It didn't end well. I lost my friends and the respect of my peers . . ." Blowing out a breath, Braylin opened her eyes to hammer her last point home. "So I made a vow to never date someone I worked with *ever* again."

Blaze frowned, but she didn't know what part of her confession he found issue with. The muscles in his jaw worked as if he clenched his teeth. His voice was rough when he spoke, "What did he do to you, Braylin?"

She stared into the blue of Blaze's eyes, amazed that the color could manage to seem so cold, as if whatever he was thinking frosted his gaze. Sighing again because she hated to reveal this part of her past, Braylin smoothed a hand along his tight jaw. "He never hurt me, at least not *physically*."

Blaze dropped a hesitant kiss along her brow, then shifted so that he lay on the cot, pulling her on top of him. His hand stroked her hair, and she let the simple movement soothe some of the shame of what she was about to admit as she molded herself around him.

"It started with little things, like criticizing my appearance in a certain outfit or cautioning me about teasing the other male pilots too much so they didn't think I was flirting."

Remembering stirred up a nasty concoction of emotions she didn't want to deal with. She felt tears prick at her eyes and blinked them furiously away. *Oh no!*

"Eventually, it got to the point where I would wait for him to approve what I was wearing before we went out, and I wouldn't even hang out with members of our unit unless he was with me." Her voice became thick with the damned tears she refused to shed. "We were together for over a year, and I . . . I lost myself."

Blaze's hand rubbed circles on her back in comfort. She held onto that as she forced the rest out on a disparaging laugh. "But that wasn't the worst of it. I'd been the best pilot in our unit, and he undermined all the hard work I'd put in to get to that position."

That fact would never not irk her. But Blaze needed to know—to know why they couldn't . . .

She pushed those thoughts away and gritted

out the part that still burned in her stomach, "Rob hadn't just wanted to control *me* but how *others* saw me. By the time I figured that out, he'd ruined my reputation and turned the whole unit against me."

Blaze's hand stilled. His voice rumbled under her cheek where she'd laid her head on his chest. "I'm sorry, Braylin. But if they couldn't see the truth of who you are, then you're better off being out."

She attempted to shrug, like her past didn't still haunt her, but her position on top of him made it awkward. "I needed a fresh start, and I found it with Leif Aero."

* * *

Blaze knew a thing or two about toxic relationships. Though Sloane had been manipulative in different ways, he'd been just as thoroughly under his ex's control, whether it had been coercing him to do what she wanted with the promise of a reward or playing the victim and blaming him for anything that went wrong in their relationship.

While his thoughts churned over everything Braylin had told him, he cradled her in his arms. This beautiful, strong, yet vulnerable woman he was falling in love with. His heart warmed with the acknowledgment, and he hugged her closer. He wanted to tell her, but something told him she wasn't ready to hear it. Instead, he turned a version of her own words on her. "*They* didn't deserve *you*."

He felt her stiffen in his arms and waited to see how she'd respond. As he played with the strands of hair tickling his chest, his mind threw his own ex in his face.

He'd thought he loved Sloane, but he'd really loved the idea of her he'd built up in his head. It took Sloane cheating on him for him to even question that idea, and even longer after the breakup, to recognize the reality of their relationship had been far from his image of it. She'd used him and manipulated him constantly. That wasn't love. He knew that for damn sure now.

Knowing the difference lit a spark of protectiveness in his bones. He wanted to hunt down this Rob asshole and beat the shit out of him for the wounds he'd caused Braylin. But more importantly, he needed to figure out how to help her heal the cuts Rob had made, or Blaze had zero chance of building a future with her.

But if she'd already broken her rules for him .

. . maybe he had a shot.

She propped herself up on an elbow and chewed her lip as she stared down at him. The expression swirling those mood-ring eyes made his heart hammer in panic. "Blaze, we can't . . . this can't be more tha—"

He could guess where her words were heading and didn't want to hear it. Desperate, he cut her off with a kiss, trying to show her how wrong she was with the press of his lips on hers. When he felt her start to relax, he rolled until their positions had reversed.

The movement freed her mouth, and Braylin opened it with an arch look. "What are you doing?"

With all her soft, smooth skin pressed against his, a wave of desire knocked him over, and he let it carry him under. Grinning, he purposefully didn't answer. He'd show her in actions, not words. Lowering his head, he figured he'd start with that spot behind her ear that made her—

He licked it, and a moan tore from her lips.

Ah, there it is.

The sweet little sound of surrender went straight to his dick. Hunger started to claw at him, and he licked his way down her body, drinking in the intoxicating taste of her. When he reached her breasts, he lavished attention on them until her nails dug into his back. The pricks of pain sent a dark and primal need surging through him. He suckled harder, making Braylin writhe beneath him.

"More!" She rocked into him, and a growl of satisfaction shook his throat.

But a fire burned in his blood, one he needed her to feel too. With her breast in his mouth, he bit down.

Her eyes flew open, and a spark branded her gaze. "Do it again."

While he switched to the other breast, he slid a finger into her dampness.

So ready.

The fire in his veins ramped up a few hundred degrees. When he nibbled on her this time, she came alive in his arms.

Like a wildcat, she rolled them, but her movement was too swift, and the cot toppled. Blaze landed on the dusty floor with Braylin on top of him. His breath had swooshed out, but he had no time to recover as he felt her hand wrap around his length. His eyes nearly rolled back in his head.

That feels fucking amazing.

But she wasted no time going for what she

needed. Blaze's eyes flew open when Braylin sheathed herself to the hilt.

"Oh God," she murmured while she rocked her hips.

Staring up at her, he could believe he'd died and gone to heaven. Her hair had half fallen out of its ponytail, and Blaze reached up, pulling the strands free from their restraining band. This time with her was all about setting themselves free—free of the past and the shadows it cast.

As if he could drive them away with his need, he gripped a hand in her hair and pulled her mouth to his. His tongue thrust in tune with his hips as his hands raced over her curves. Craving, touching, marking.

She gasped when he spanked her, and their mouths broke apart, the sound of furious panting filling the small tower room. The look she gave him promised retribution, and he welcomed it.

Flesh slapped against flesh as he gripped her hips and drove her faster, chasing the wildfire that had been burning between them since the day they'd met.

"Blaze," Braylin groaned his name, and hearing it made him wild. He rolled them until he could pound into her, thrusting deeper until he felt her spasm around him.

Dark, blinding pleasure overtook him, and he howled, hammering into her until he broke. Thoroughly spent, he collapsed on top of her in an exhausted heap.

When he could move his arms, he shifted, pulling Braylin on top of him and off the dirty floor. He pressed a kiss to her temple. The words of love filling his chest danced excitedly on his tongue, wanting to spill out of his mouth, but he swallowed them. He'd save them for when she wanted to hear them.

With both of them sated, Blaze felt hulled-out and bare as the earth after a prescribed burn. Empty but made new again. He stroked a hand up Braylin's back and smiled at the wooden ceiling. *Home.* With her, he'd found his home.

CHAPTER 16

Personal Protective Equipment

By the time they made it off the floor, the light had faded as the hours bled into the afternoon. And Braylin had set absolutely *zero* boundaries.

Seriously, what's wrong with me?

Her stomach roiled with each moment of indecision. She was half elation over everything she and Blaze had shared and half dread. More than once, as they'd searched for the batteries they needed to get the radio working, she'd opened her mouth to make things clear, only to shut it again.

Blaze had asked her to trust him, and if she was honest with herself, she did. But the little voice in her subconscious that still cowered over her past mistakes liked to remind her she'd trusted Rob, too.

That's how he'd been able to hurt her so thoroughly.

It might not be fair to compare Blaze with her bastard of an ex, but it didn't stop her from doing it.

Damn you, Rob.

When she pinched her finger in the metal stand for the solar panels, she cursed and shook off the tendrils of the past clinging to her like mist over a pond.

She and Blaze had found all the components they needed to get the radio working; they just had to piece them back together. What they worked at now was securing the panels to the solar tracker they'd found. It and the batteries had been in a metal cargo case half-shoved behind the desk downstairs. She'd noticed it while they'd been lying on the floor. Instead of tackling her feelings, she'd pointed out the case instead.

I'm such a coward.

Annoyed with herself and frowning because of it, Braylin held the stand where Blaze directed while he attached one of the two-by-four-feet solar panels. The tracker was a stand that would move the panels with the sun and provide as much charging time as possible. Considering they'd wasted half the day's rays, that was kind of important.

Not that she regretted how they'd spent the day. She *should*. But she didn't. In fact, she had a few ideas on how they could pass the time it would take for the panels to charge the batteries. Just imagining it, her body hummed in anticipation.

"Damn!" Blaze's curse pulled her from the salacious turn of her thoughts.

"What is it?" When the question came out in a high-pitched tone, her face heated with guilt over being caught thinking about him.

"The tracker's broken." His head popped around the front side of the panel to meet her gaze. "We're going to have to just set them up on the ground."

That was less than ideal, but as long as they could still generate enough juice to power the radio, she wouldn't complain. "Whatever works."

He gave her a strange look like he'd expected her to argue.

Okay, she could admit the majority of the time they'd known each other, she'd more often been combative than not, but she knew how to be agreeable.

When she said nothing else, he disappeared around the panel again. "As soon as I lift them off, move the stand out of the way, okay?"

Clearly, Blaze held some sort of sway over her—*must be the sex*—because she'd willingly dropped her defenses around him. "Copy."

When the panels no longer blocked her view of the forest, Braylin's eye caught on a tuft of brown fur that glued her feet to the ground. "Oh, God. It's back."

"What?" Blaze held the panels in front of his face, waiting for her to move the stand she'd forgotten about in her fear.

"The moose!" she hissed under her breath as if the thing could hear them from a hundred yards away. It stood at the edge of the forest as still as a statue.

"Braylin, grab the stand."

"What?" She didn't understand why he sounded annoyed with her when the moose was the issue.

"The stand! These things are getting heavy."

"Oh, sorry!" She snatched the tracker from underneath, where he still held the panels aloft and turned back to ensure the moose hadn't moved.

It hadn't. The knot in her stomach eased a fraction.

Blaze began maneuvering the solar panels into

the best position to catch the sunlight, oblivious to her freaking out. Braylin would've rolled her eyes at him, but she couldn't blink. She and the animal were in a standoff. "How do we get rid of it?"

"Get rid of what?"

"Blaze! You're not listening. The moose is back!" Loads of rocks littered the ground between it and them. Maybe throwing some would scare it away? Or would that only make it angry and send it charging at them again?

While she tried to come up with a battle plan, Blaze started laughing. It surprised her enough to turn away from the beast. "What could possibly be funny about this?"

"That's not a moose. It's an elk."

"An elk?" She gave the animal another look, squinting to see better. "How can you tell?"

"Different type of antlers. Plus, look at the body. It's more deer than horse-like."

Okay, yes, she'd give him that. This one actually did look like an oversized deer, but after her last experience, she wasn't taking chances with anything that had antlers. "Will it go away?"

"Most likely."

While she stood there worrying her lip, Blaze's arms came around her. "I promise that guy's not a threat."

He kissed the top of her head, and the simple gesture made her smile. He'd become very affectionate over the last few hours, or maybe he'd always been that way; she'd just never let him show it before.

The thought seared her chest, branding her with panic.

What am I doing?

* * *

Drowning. That's what Braylin was doing. By now, the quicksand had reached her chin, and she still hadn't tried to pull herself out of it.

Well, she'd tried, but not very hard. Every time she'd broached the subject of where things were going, Blaze managed to distract her. The man had magic everything: lips, hands, cock. Whenever she opened her mouth to tell him she couldn't have a relationship with him, he touched her or kissed her until they wound up back on the cot, or the floor, or against the windows. There was no part of the tower they hadn't christened.

Staring at his profile, Braylin sighed. They'd made a bench out of the cargo case and were using it to watch the evening fall. His tousled hair shifted in the breeze, and her chest ached like too many warring emotions were battling it out in there. The problem she faced was that what she wanted existed in opposition to the rules she'd set for herself.

What if things with Blaze could work out?

But as much as she'd like to feed the hope that sprouted with the question, the shadows of her past moved in and blocked any chance at light.

What if they don't?

She didn't know if she could survive another hit like the one she'd taken from Rob. She was running out of places and jobs to start over with if she intended to keep flying.

Blaze caught her staring and smiled, pulling her into his side with an arm around her middle. He'd stopped wearing the sling on his other arm, but she wouldn't chastise him about it. Even if she did kind of miss the Indiana Jones look.

She gave a soft chuckle and relaxed against his shoulder, tilting her head to watch the sky. The sun had just started to descend, painting the world around them in effervescent pinks, oranges, and purples. Watching the colors bleed across the distant peaks, she thought it might be the prettiest sunset she'd ever seen. Not that she had a habit of watching them, but it made for an impressive sight at this elevation. Almost as if they were a part of the sunset instead of simply glimpsing it from afar.

A loud bleating tore through the air, slicing the calm into ribbons. They both bolted upright.

"What the heck was that?" she asked over the thundering of her heart.

"It sounded like . . ." Blaze trailed off into a frown, and she followed his gaze.

Are those sheep?

A dozen or more horned animals broke from the tree line, and Braylin instinctively stepped back. They seemed . . . *panicked.* "What's going on?"

The herd of sheep scrambled away from the forest, which meant they headed straight up the rise to the tower.

"Let's go." Blaze had grabbed the binoculars from the desk inside and now tugged her toward the stairs leading to the tower's top level. She climbed as he talked. "Those are bighorn sheep. They're fleeing something, and I don't think it's a larger predator."

Realization dawned, and her stomach hardened with dread. "The fire?"

Blaze didn't say anything—because he didn't have to. They reached the deck, walking around to the side facing the forest. A growing column of smoke visible even without the binoculars marred the sunset-painted sky.

How did it get so close so fast?

Even as she wondered about it, Blaze spoke. "The wind shifted. It's blowing the fire uphill, right at us." He tucked the weather meter he'd just consulted back into his pants pocket.

"What do we do?" Though she didn't notice, her question came out barely over a whisper. That strange, choking feeling had taken over her chest again.

They were stuck, and a wildfire raged toward them.

"Braylin, look at me." She blinked, focusing on the calm timbre of Blaze's voice, and found her cheeks squished between his palms. "Focus on your breathing. Don't think about anything else." His eyes were soft with concern, and they almost made her smile. "Just in and out, okay?"

She thought she managed a nod before she did as he asked.

"We're going to radio for help. Then we'll be off this mountain before the fire gets anywhere near us," he reassured her.

Right! The radio. They weren't trapped. Not this time. Her heart rate started to settle, but she kept pulling in deep breaths, holding them, and letting them out slowly.

He'd released her face, but his gaze never left her while she cut off the flow of panic trying to weaken her. She found gaining control came easier this time, and as she felt it subside, she gave him a small smile in appreciation. "Thank you."

How was he always so in tune with her, knowing exactly what she needed?

His hand cupped the back of her neck, pulling her close as he placed a tender kiss on her forehead. She felt herself slipping deeper into the quicksand, and her hands gripped his shirt collar. To hold him there or stop herself from sinking— she wasn't sure.

* * *

The solar panels had gotten around five hours of sunlight, giving the batteries just enough charge to power the radio. As soon as it had glowed with life, Braylin made a call for help on the forest service channels until they received a response.

Now, all they had to do was wait and hope the fire didn't reach them before the rescue helicopter. They sat on the open top deck, their feet dangling through the railing. The sheep had invaded the area around the tower's base, and their anxious noises—a weird coughing sound—

filled the night air.

Maybe it was the nervousness rolling off the animals or the realization that their little fantasy world was about to come to an end, but Braylin's whole body tensed as if for a fight. If she were going to clear things up with Blaze, this would be her last chance. She chewed her lip and tried not to notice how often he checked the weather meter.

Even if she wanted to risk taking the leap and accept she had feelings for him, she wouldn't jump without a parachute. There was no guarantee that things wouldn't turn sour, and since they worked together, she couldn't take that chance.

Fear finally motivated her enough to speak. "Blaze . . ." Fuck, she practically choked on his name. Swallowing around the knot in her throat, Braylin tried again.

He pushed a lock of hair behind her ear. "What is it, angel?"

As much as she didn't want to, she owed it to him to at least look him in the eye for this. Taking a deep breath, she met his midnight gaze. Somehow, the blue still managed to shine in the dark, like he was lit by some inner spark.

Her resolve wavered, but cold fingers of fear squeezed the words out of her. "The past few days have been . . ." *Wonderful, but they're a fantasy.* Grim reality waited to smack her in the face. She reached for his hand and gave it a desperate squeeze. "Promise me you won't tell anyone about us, that we, you know." Dammit, now her face was on fire.

Blaze didn't grin at her inability to say the words 'had sex' like she'd thought he would. Instead, his face was expressionless—utterly blank.

When he didn't respond, a different kind of panic started to crawl over her skin in wave after wave of itchy invasion. Trying to ignore it, she pushed on. "We work together. I won't let this time with you ruin my reputation or my job. If you want to continue sleeping together, we can. But it's *just* sex." Because she worried it needed to be restated, she added, "And you can't tell anyone about us."

Was it a trick of the waning light, or did the spark in his eyes dim?

There should've been relief that she'd finally set the boundaries she'd wanted to, but all Braylin could feel was hollow. Like she'd ripped away anything solid between them.

When the silence stretched, more empty voids formed within her until she became as pockmarked as an underground cave.

* * *

Blaze's heart shattered from the blow of her words. The jagged pieces it broke into should've hurt, cutting him wherever they landed, but he couldn't feel a thing. She'd smothered the fire that burned between them with a line of retardant, and the cloying pink spray settled over him in a heavy, numbing cloud.

He shouldn't have been surprised; he'd known this was coming. Yet hearing the words still took him off guard because he'd let himself hope he had managed to change her mind.

Not even close.

The thought had him shaking his head. It was good he'd been sitting down, or the disappointment might've knocked him on his ass.

"Blaze?" She squeezed the hand she gripped, her mood-ring eyes imploring him for a response.

But what could he say? *Thanks anyway, angel?*

Because he wouldn't settle for *just* sex. He wanted more, *deserved* more. And so did Braylin. Why couldn't she see that?

The last few days felt like a lifetime. He'd gotten to know her—her past and her faults. None of it scared him. He wanted all sides of her because he'd never met someone who matched him so completely. Neither of them was perfectly formed.

Hell, they both wore PPE when it came to their past relationships. Like his flame-resistant clothing or her flight helmet, they'd donned personal protective equipment as shields to guard against the wounds they carried. But they'd lowered them for each other during their time on the mountain. Where Braylin was concave, he was convex. They fit with one another like two pieces of the same puzzle, and they could only be whole when they stuck together.

And she was going to throw all of that away.

She doesn't trust me.

She must not if she wasn't willing to have a relationship outside the bedroom. The realization was another blow to Blaze's heart. It penetrated the numbing fog, and he grimaced against the pain, pulling his hand free of hers. The loss of contact only intensified the hurt, spreading it with a searing heat that squeezed his lungs tight enough to choke off his air supply.

Like a switch flipping, night fell, and he welcomed the darkness, wishing it could soothe some of the heart splinters shredding his insides.

He heard Braylin's soft gasp of surprise at how quickly they were plunged into the abyss, and his first instinct was to reassure her.

No matter that she'd hurt him, he *loved* her.

Blaze opened his mouth, ready to beg if that's what it took, but a familiar whop drowned out his words. They heard the helicopter's blades first. Then its searchlight lit up the tower.

He climbed to his feet, shielding his face with an arm as the light nearly blinded him. The startled bighorns fled down the rocky cliff face behind the tower, finally realizing they'd had a safe path of escape from the wildfire all along. It was too steep for human passage without climbing gear, but the sheep nimbly traversed the jagged terrain urged on by some primal instinct.

Maybe that's what fueled him now. A primal urge to protect himself—to keep from being manipulated into an agreement he didn't want. The way Sloane had so often done. Because instead of telling Braylin how he felt while they waited for the rescue helicopter to land, he didn't say anything. At all.

CHAPTER 17

Blaze of Glory

Blaze robbed her of sleep. But *not* in the way Braylin would've wished. They could have been sharing her king-sized bed right now, but he'd said no to her terms. Or at least, she'd interpreted his *lack* of response in the negative.

After being rescued, they were taken to the hospital. He'd said nothing on the ride back to civilization, and then, as soon as they'd landed, she'd been led one way and him another.

She hadn't seen him since.

The doctor had given her a clean bill of health. Apart from the fading bruises, her ribs were fine. But not knowing how Blaze fared continued to eat at her until sleep became impossible.

She'd gotten used to sleeping in the pitch-black darkness of the wilderness, and the streetlight outside her apartment cast shadows that flickered across her bedroom ceiling. Staring up at them, she let out a frustrated huff and kicked the sheets off. Not knowing about Blaze's injuries wasn't the only thing eating at her.

Why didn't he say anything?

It hurt worse for some reason. Not being worthy of an answer or even an excuse. She would've taken either from him and been fine. Shrugged it off and moved on, right?

But to leave me with nothing . . .

Like picking at a scab, she kept replaying the conversation, trying to understand where she'd gone wrong. But he'd given her no clues, no indication as to what he thought about her proposal, *except* when he'd taken his hand from hers. The sting of his dismissal still reverberated. It had started an ache in her chest that spread outward like a shockwave.

Damn you, Blaze.

In a jerky move, Braylin sat up, tossing her legs over the side of the bed. If she couldn't sleep, she could work. She still had an incident report to write up about the crash.

Her boss had met her at the hospital and had shown genuine relief to see her in one piece. Dale hadn't even seemed upset about the loss of the aircraft. Instead, he'd praised her skills for landing it safely. But she'd read between the lines and knew he wanted the report as soon as possible. *Or* her guilt over letting the helicopter burn to a crisp was what pushed her to get it done.

She reached for her phone on the bedside table and noted it was ten-thirty. The hangar would likely be empty, giving her plenty of quiet to finish the write-up of the accident.

With a nod of resolve, Braylin started to get dressed. Even if her boss hadn't pushed for the report, it would give her something other than Blaze to focus on, and right now, she needed that. Desperately.

* * *

Blaze strolled into Backyard Barb's around eleven and snagged a stool at the crowded bar. The din of voices drowned out the typical country music blaring over the speakers as he signaled Barb for a drink.

He didn't think Braylin would be here, but it didn't stop him from looking. A wide range of patrons packed the place, from the barely legal to the senior citizen discounters, but no matter how hard his eyes scanned, they didn't land on a gorgeous brunette with multi-colored hazel eyes.

With a sigh, he looked for Barb and nearly jumped with surprise to find her standing right before him. How long had he been searching for Braylin?

Pushing the thought away, he forced a smile. "It's rowdy in here tonight."

Her answering grin came and went so fast that he almost missed it. "Sure is, sugar. What'll it be?"

"I'll take a Coors draft."

"Be right back." She winked before she turned away to pull his beer, and the smile that crossed his face this time felt more genuine.

But despite his lips curving, a dullness permeated Blaze's chest. Maybe it was regret over the way he'd left things with Braylin. Whatever it was, he wasn't ready to face it yet.

Barb sat his drink on the bar with a lifted brow. "I hear you're the luckiest S.O.B. alive."

Blaze had just taken a sip of his beer and had to swallow hard. "What?"

"Survived a chopper crash, didn't you?" She nodded at the sling he wore.

A rueful smile twisted his lips. He'd gotten an earful at the hospital about not keeping his injured shoulder immobilized. Then the doctor ordered him to wear the sling for the next week—

at least.

"I don't think that had anything to do with luck," he told Barb, trying and failing not to picture Braylin and how she'd kept them both from splattering on the mountainside like bugs on a windshield.

He hadn't seen her since they'd landed at the hospital. In fact, he felt like the *unluckiest* son-of-a-bitch alive since she'd walked away from him. The goal in coming here had been to put Braylin out of his mind, but she haunted every other thought. *Dammit.*

Blaze was frowning at nothing when Barb's laugh pulled him back into the present and away from the shitstorm of the last few hours.

"Where is she?" Barb asked now.

He blinked, worried he'd missed something else Barb had said. "Where's who?"

The aging blonde propped a hand on her hip and gave him a look that said, 'Are you really that dumb?' before she opened her mouth and explained, "The woman you're mopin' about."

Blaze didn't think he was *moping*. A scowl hardened his brow, but he kept his voice even. "Have you ever been in love, Barb?"

Her expression went from teasing to sympathetic as she patted his hand. "It's the best and worst feeling." Leaning back, she crossed her arms on the bar. "Did you tell her how you feel?"

The question made him wince. Dropping her gaze, he shook his head.

Would it have made a difference?

He didn't know the answer, and fear that it wouldn't have, kept him from telling Braylin the words bouncing around his chest. Leaving them unspoken had turned them into projectiles. Wherever they hit, they left a dull ache behind.

A smack landed on the top of his head, and Blaze reared back in his seat. He rubbed the spot while he stared wide-eyed at Barb. "What was that for?"

"For being a coward." Her blue eyes glittered with steel. "Now finish that pint, man up, and go get your girl."

Blaze sat speechless as she whirled away in a huff of heavy perfume. Thoroughly chastised, he sipped his beer and wondered if Barb was right. Had he been a coward?

Remembering how he hadn't spoken a word to Braylin after she'd broken his heart did seem like a cop-out. Blaze couldn't account for how he'd acted or, really, *not* acted, except that he had to have been in shock.

Things had been so good he hadn't wanted to

think about the possibility she might not want what he wanted. And when he'd had the opportunity to convince her otherwise, he'd stayed silent. Walked away without a word like a . . . *coward*.

Ah, fuck.

He had to find Braylin.

* * *

Braylin was poring over maintenance records when she heard the hangar door slide open. With a sigh, she scrubbed at her eyes and checked the time. She'd been at it for nearly an hour.

Who's coming into the hangar this late?

Maybe one of the maintainers had forgotten something. She wasn't thrilled about the interruption, but a break could be good.

Yawning, she stood up and stretched. She had almost finished the incident report when it occurred to her to check the maintenance logbook for anything that might have caused the crash. Since they'd had fuel, but the engine had died, logically, that meant the fuel hadn't been getting to the engine. So Braylin started her search for answers by looking at any repairs completed on the aircraft's fuel system.

Her best guess was there had been an issue

with the fuel line, but she'd checked it herself the morning of the crash. Looking back through the logs reminded her of the problem she'd noticed the day she'd confronted Roger, too. Where the gauge hadn't given her an accurate reading on how much fuel had been in the tank. She didn't know if the one had anything to do with the other, but her gut told her the fuel system had to be the reason for the crash.

When she'd conducted her inspection the morning of the accident, the flexible hose that carried fuel from the tank to the engine had been connected, and the striping of indicator paste on it remained unbroken. The paste they used in the hangar was called torque seal, and it served as a visual marker. If the seal was broken, something had either been tampered with or, more likely, it had come loose from the vibrations caused by flight. Even though the fuel line had been secure as far as she could tell, something about it bugged her, and Braylin kept asking herself the same question.

What did I miss?

Or did Roger miss something? Seeing his signature on every one of the latest maintenance entries made her heart ache. Her former crew chief was one more reason she needed to protect herself. Despite how good they might seem, people couldn't be trusted. Her stomach burned in protest over the bitter turn of her thoughts, but she ignored it.

Thinking about how Roger lied to her and went behind the company's back, selling their parts, helped her accept she'd made the right decision with Blaze. She'd offered him more than she should've since they worked together. They could've stayed friends with benefits, but if he didn't want to take her up on it, that was fine. She was probably better off.

Nodding her head in defiance of the hollowness in her chest, Braylin left the office to see who had opened the bay door.

* * *

Blaze hadn't really expected Braylin to be at the hangar after midnight, so his heart tripped in surprise at seeing the bay door slid open. When he climbed out of his truck and drew closer, he frowned. The door was open, but the lights weren't on. Had someone simply forgotten to close it?

He stepped inside. While he waited for his eyes to adjust from the dimness inside the hangar, the beam of a flashlight caught his attention. It bounced off the racks in the back that held spare helicopter parts.

Maybe the power's out?

Wondering if it was Braylin or someone who needed help, he started to call out when a sense of unease prickled the back of his neck. Braylin's voice and another he didn't recognize but didn't like the sound of reached his ears. They were coming from the offices.

Some instinct cautioned him to keep to the shadows as he crept around helicopters until he moved close enough to hear their conversation.

"Roger's not here." A light from one of the offices backlit Braylin, where she stood with her arms crossed.

Oh, shit. Was this about her gambling crew chief?

His whole body tensed while his veins surged with adrenaline. Whoever had come looking for Roger couldn't be good.

The other voice spoke. It belonged to a man in a dark suit and sounded as oily as a seedy car dealer. "I'm aware of that, sweetheart, but he still owes Mr. Arnaud a lot of money. The boss doesn't take kindly to people who don't pay back their loans." The man paused, and a smile crept into his voice. "Sometimes an example needs to be set."

"What do you mean by 'an example'?" Braylin's voice and demeanor screamed 'calm,' but Blaze operated at the opposite end of that spectrum.

Every muscle in his body vibrated with restrained energy. His system was as charged as it would be with a wildfire breathing down his neck. He wished he had his cellphone to call for help, but he hadn't gotten a replacement for the one that burned up in the chopper.

"Accidents, sweetheart." The man shrugged. "They happen all the time, especially when it comes to helicopter maintenance . . ."

Blaze felt Braylin's anger when she hissed, "You had something to do with the crash?"

"Maybe we did, but the paper trail will show Roger's to blame for that. Now, tell me where he is."

"I don't know. And if I did, I wouldn't tell you."

Don't piss this guy off, Braylin!

Oily Asshole didn't like her response. He took a step closer, and Blaze's stomach dropped to the floor at the sight of the gun in the man's hand.

Oh fuck. But at least it wasn't pointed at Braylin.

"Hmm, if you don't help us find Roger, we could just let *you* pay off his debt." The man's hand reached for her cheek, and she jerked away. He laughed, then added with a sneer, "A sweet face on a body like yours, and Mr. Arnaud would have his money back in no time."

Okay, Blaze had heard enough. This slimy fucker needed to back the hell away from his woman. He unhooked the sling from his shoulder and let it fall to the floor with a silent apology to his doctor.

About to do something reckless, Blaze paused when the light coming through the office door glinted off a shiny piece of metal and caught his eye.

A torque wrench.

It might not be the best weapon against the other man's gun, but it would be better than nothing. He swiped it from the rolling tool cart as he passed. It was a one-inch wrench and had some weight. The bit end looked large enough to serve as a club . . . should he need it.

Holding the wrench behind his back, Blaze stepped out of the shadows. He gritted his teeth against the pounding in his ears and worked hard at keeping his voice nonthreatening. "Hey, man. It looks like you're trespassing."

"Blaze," Braylin gasped, her face paling.

Not exactly the reaction he'd hoped for, but

they'd hash things out after he ensured she was safe. That's all that mattered now.

Oily Asshole whirled and raised his weapon. "Blaze, huh? That's your name?" He pointed the gun at Blaze's heart. "You should've left well enough alone. But if you want to play hero, you're going to go out in . . . what's that saying?" The demented bastard grinned. "Oh yeah, a Blaze of Glory."

Anticipating the shot and without a second thought, Blaze rushed the man, swinging the wrench at the hand that held the gun.

"Aargh!" The oily bastard howled in pain as the weapon flew out of his grip.

Before he had a chance to recover, Blaze swung again. With the ease of slinging an ax on the job, he hit the man square in the temple, tipping him over like a felled log.

"Oh my God." Braylin stared down at the now unconscious man at her feet.

Relief wanted to flood in, but they weren't out of the woods yet. Blaze grabbed Braylin in a quick squeeze, needing to hold her and assure himself she was okay.

She's not hurt.

In fact, neither of them sported bullet holes, so they were doing pretty well. He kissed the top of her head and then pushed her back to arm's length. "Barricade yourself in the office and call the police."

He didn't wait to see if she complied. The person with the flashlight was Blaze's concern now. If Braylin were going to be safe, he had to find this fucker. Whoever they were probably had a weapon and had likely heard Oily's yelp.

Blaze merged with the shadows as he made his way to the back of the hangar. The flashlight beam had been extinguished, leaving him at a loss for the other person's location. Searching the rows of shelving, he strained over the rapid beating of his own heart to hear footsteps or breathing that would clue him into the other man's presence.

"Blaze!"

At Braylin's shout, his breath seized in his chest, and he rushed back to the hangar's offices. Instead of being hidden inside as he'd ordered her, she stood over Oily Asshole, pointing a gun at the other perpetrator.

"What the hell, Braylin?" he growled in frustrated relief.

On closer inspection, she'd zip-tied the oily man's hands and feet and now held the gun on his friend like it was second nature. "Kneel."

Blaze didn't see a weapon on the man Braylin

spoke to, and not knowing made his skin too tight. Worry crawled under it like a thousand bark beetles. He clenched the wrench in his hand, ready to use it if need be.

When the man did as she ordered, she glanced at Blaze. "Grab the zip ties and secure him."

This bastard was bigger, clearly the muscle of the operation, and he didn't like being ordered around by a woman. He had a scar on his left cheek that stretched into a gruesome sight when he sneered at Braylin. "You're gonna regret this, bitch."

Blaze tied the asshole's hands together tight enough to cut off his circulation. "Don't call her that," he warned under his breath.

The bastard laughed. "Or what? You're both going to die. Mr. Arnaud wil—"

When the vitriol stopped abruptly, Blaze looked up from where he'd been securing the man's feet to see Braylin scowling down at the fucker.

"Did you just . . ."

"I was tired of listening to him." She'd knocked the man out with the butt of the gun she held.

Blaze wasn't sure if he should be impressed or afraid. "Did he have a weapon?" He was ready to start patting the man down, but Braylin spoke.

"I'm holding it. The other one's over there somewhere." She gestured like it wasn't a big deal, but that didn't make Blaze's stomach any less hard.

The fear that had gripped him since he'd first seen the man holding a gun refused to go away. It strangled his voice as he pushed to his feet. "I told you to stay safe and call for help."

She shrugged. "I did. But I couldn't stay locked in there and leave you out here with these idiots."

So amazingly strong. Blaze admired that strength even if it aged him ten years. She'd put herself in danger—for him. He hadn't needed this situation to remind him tomorrow was never a guarantee, especially when they both held hazardous jobs. But he wanted to spend as many of those tomorrows as he could with Braylin.

He had to tell her. "Bray—"

Oily Idiot stirred, coming to with a groan that robbed Blaze of his chance. When the man tried to reach for his—no doubt—aching head and found he couldn't, his eyes popped wide. "Who the hell *are* you?"

Before Blaze could answer, growing sirens echoed through the hangar. He grinned, and it was full of malice. "We're wildland firefighters, asshole."

CHAPTER 18

Reborn from the Ashes

Tired enough to be delirious, Braylin couldn't be sure she wasn't dreaming. It didn't help that the night's events had a surreal quality about them. She'd wanted to discover what caused the aircraft to crash but hadn't expected *sabotage*.

While they'd waited for help to arrive, she'd pulled the truth from the asshole who seemed to be the leader of Mr. Arnaud's men. Hearing him talk about maintenance accidents made her realize what had been bothering her about the helicopter's fuel system. When she'd checked it the morning of the crash, the striping that covered the fuel line connector had been yellow. The indicator paste came in different colors, but Leif Aero's maintenance crews usually used orange.

She'd bet whatever money Roger owed these goons that they loosened the fuel line and then re-striped it so she wouldn't notice anything amiss.

With the fuel line loosened it would've eventually come off from the vibrations caused during flight. Without that connection, the fuel wouldn't get to the engine, which would cause it to suck in air and flame out.

Just like it did before the accident.

And with Roger's signature on the most recent maintenance repair for the fuel system, the blame would have fallen on him.

If the crash had gone differently . . . that might've been retribution for Mr. Arnaud, but she and Blaze were a wrench in their plans. She snorted, almost dopey from lack of sleep, as she thought of Blaze saving the day with a torque wrench. Though when he'd appeared out of nowhere, he'd nearly given her a heart attack.

Braylin gave a weary sigh and rubbed at her temple. She'd told everything she'd found out to her boss. His was one of the cacophony of voices filling the hangar. Several police officers and people she didn't recognize crowded the lounge area of the hangar where they'd parked her and Blaze to get their statements.

Even though she hadn't needed to use her self-defense skills against an armed attacker since she'd learned them while in the Army, she was glad her body hadn't forgotten how. Disarming the second man had been too easy; his kind rarely expected women to fight back.

A satisfied smile tilted her lips. It had probably helped that Mr. Arnaud's men thoroughly pissed her off, first, by being responsible for the crash that could've killed her, then by threatening to shoot Blaze. Her smile faded. Seeing a gun pointed at his chest had been a revelation for her. As painful and permanent as a hot brand on her heart.

She was in love with him.

But he hurt me.

She'd lowered her defenses for him without realizing it, and he'd hurt her. Acknowledging that clanged through the hollow bits inside her, spreading dullness in their wake.

Braylin blinked as people fired questions at her, but all she could focus on was the need to talk to Blaze. He sat in a chair across the room from her. Someone had put a sling on his injured arm, but it didn't stop him from using it as he gestured to a police officer.

Several things occurred to her as she stared, trickling in like sand through an hourglass. The arm in the sling was the same one he'd used to wield the wrench. She hoped he hadn't made the injury worse, but she couldn't seem to find the will to be angry with him about it. The predominant emotion she felt was relief. It had made her muscles weak enough that when they asked her to sit, she'd slid bonelessly into the hard plastic chairs lining the walls in a 'U.'

He could've died.

The shock of seeing Blaze had worn off, and her heart ached as she watched him scoop the blonde locks away that had fallen into his face.

Why did he come back?

Dale's voice penetrated her fog, and she glanced up to see her boss pat her shoulder. "Go home, Whit. We'll square the rest of this away tomorrow."

"Thank you, sir." The words were an automatic response and felt wooden in her mouth.

Her gaze went back to Blaze when she forced herself to her feet. He watched her, and something in his eyes made her feel like she walked the plank. Would he catch her if she plunged off, or did shark-infested waters wait for her at the bottom?

I love you. You hurt me. You hurt me. I love

you.

The two sentences competed in her head, and she couldn't seem to untangle them enough to speak. With a shudder, she looked away, forcing one foot in front of the other as she left the hangar.

A gentle night breeze stroked her face, sending scents of the valley across her cheeks, but Blaze was the only thing she could smell. Smoke and birchwood, his scent had singed her nose and refused to go away.

"Braylin, wait!" Blaze caught her before she reached her car. She'd parked under a parking lamp, and its glow created a cone in the darkness.

Though she paused, she couldn't turn. She was used to protecting herself, but right now, her defenses were as fragile as cracked glass. One well-aimed blow, and they'd crumble to pieces.

His hand gently grasped her arm. Then he turned her around. "Braylin . . ."

Her eyes stuck on his shoulder, but his palm slid up her neck, tilting her face to meet his.

"Angel," the word murmured over her skin like a caress, and his eyes were so soft hers welled with tears.

Blinking them away, she asked, "What are you doing here, Blaze?"

"Looking for you."

"How'd you know I was here?"

His thumb traced circles on her temple, and she tried and failed not to lean into him. "I didn't. But I hoped you were. I wanted to talk to you, and I don't know where your apartment is."

You hurt me. The memory made her voice come out with a bite. "There's such a thing as a phone, you know."

"Not for this. I needed to see you, to say . . ."—his voice cracked—"what I wanted to say. In person."

The glass of her protective walls started to tremble under his touch, and she lashed out with the last defense she had—anger. "You seemed fine before with giving me the silent treatment."

"I know." His hand dropped from her face with a weary sigh. "I'm sorry." Then his eyes speared her, and the pain in them echoed her own. "But you hurt me."

I did, but . . . "How?" His admission snaked across her walls in a hairline fracture, weakening them further. "I thought you'd want—"

Blaze cut her off with a growl. "I want you, Braylin. Not just your body but all of you." The spark in his gaze sent her heart beating unnaturally fast. "I want the feisty Amazon that likes to bust my balls." A grin flashed and was gone. "The woman who can take down an armed man with her bare hands and the helicopter pilot that slings water like a pro." He stepped toward her, his knuckles brushing her cheek as he crooned, "And the vulnerable parts that hide under your shield. All of it." His face softened into a smile. "My angel in the sky."

A sob nearly hiccupped out of her. *I love you.*

While her eyes swam with unshed tears, the words rammed against her fortifications, but fear stopped them from breaking free. She wanted all of Blaze, too, but could she take the risk? Would being with him be worth it?

A war raged within her, and Braylin covered her mouth with the back of her hand, trying to hold back the tears threatening to shake her body in their battle to be released.

Blaze pulled it away and held on. "I love you, Braylin."

Her eyes met his, and the hesitation she glimpsed, as if he thought she'd hurt him again, snapped something inside her. Her defenses crumbled into a thousand pointless pieces.

What am I doing?

It was time to stop letting her past relationship rob her of the opportunity to pursue a new one.

She owed it to herself and to Blaze.

A slow, watery smile lit her whole face as the warmth building in her chest told her she'd finally thrown off the heavy mantle of her past. "I love you too."

Blaze's eyes darkened. Then he shucked off the sling and pulled her against him. Capturing her face in both palms, he rasped, "Say it again."

A soggy chuckle bubbled up her throat. "I love you, Blaze."

His chest rose with a deep, savoring breath before he lowered his forehead to hers and murmured, "My angel."

Euphoria washed over her in a daze. She'd dared to walk the plank, and he'd caught her instead of feeding her to the sharks. Reaching up, she tilted his head to join their lips. The first touch sparked a fire between them.

Hot enough to soothe old wounds and heal new ones, Blaze crushed his mouth to hers in a kiss full of everything they'd been through together. It spoke of hurt and fear but ended with the softest brushing of tongues—a promise to build a future on. She welcomed it.

Their lips parted, and breaths mingled. Transfixed, she could only stare in wonder. They were two hearts beating as one, scorched by the fire of their love and reborn from the ashes like a phoenix rising against the sun. Ready to forge a new path in the black.

As Braylin gazed into the deep blue sea of Blaze's eyes, love filled the holes in her heart, making her beam with joy. "Come home with me?" she whispered.

As if he didn't need a second invitation, Blaze grinned and made her stomach dance with pleasure. "I thought you'd never ask."

EPILOGUE

Five Months Later

Braylin cracked open the driver's side window and let the crisp autumn air filter into the car as she drove home from the hangar. Mountains covered in a riot of fall colors filled her rear-view window and made her smile. The trees down either side of the highway she whizzed by broadcasted those same changing leaves. Yellow, orange, and red blended together into a mixture of paints on the palette of nature.

While they were gorgeous in their own right, Braylin's smile beamed because of what those colors signaled—the close of fire season.

Leif Aero's contracts with the Forest Service had ended for the year, and she'd just parked the aircraft in the hangar for its winter overhaul, which meant she had a glorious few months off. And she knew exactly how she planned to spend them . . . or, at least, who she intended to spend them *with*.

Thinking of Blaze still made her stomach flutter. He had gone back to his crew after he'd been cleared from his shoulder injury, but they'd been able to see each other at the end of his rolls, spending most of that time locked in her apartment.

She snickered, remembering how often they'd made love, barely coming up for air and only when she became too hangry. It had been like that for the week immediately following their run-in with Mr. Arnaud's men, too.

Her boss had given her some days off after she'd finally written up the after-action report for the training she'd been conducting with Blaze, culminating in its unceremonious end. The helicopter might've gone up in flames, but it had been the spark that started the blaze of their relationship.

A contented sigh left Braylin's lips. Feelings, she'd come to realize, weren't such a bad thing to catch, after all.

I can't wait to see him!

The drought had finally broken a few weeks

ago, and though Blaze's crew had fought fires all over the western U.S. the past few months, today marked the last day of his last roll for the season. He'd be home tonight.

Knowing she'd see him in a few short hours never failed to make her giddy. She felt so light and buoyant she hardly needed the aircraft to fly. For months, she'd been floating on a cloud of complete and utter bliss. She was so happy it was disgusting.

Braylin snort-laughed then screeched when she had to slam on brakes as a deer hopped across the road. As she slowed, the buck managed to cross both lanes unharmed. She took a deep breath and hit the accelerator. Clearly, animals with antlers still had it in for her.

When her phone started to ring, she stopped glaring at the deer to glance at the caller's I.D.

Roger.

Braylin didn't pick up. She was in too good a mood to try and soothe her former crew chief out of whatever funk he'd hit now. Finding out about what caused her to crash and what nearly happened to her at the hangar with Mr. Arnaud's men had been enough to scare Roger straight. He'd helped build a case against the men who'd broken in and started going to Gamblers

Anonymous to get his life back on track.

A frown tugged at her lips. She was truly happy Roger had gotten help for his addiction, but he'd started apologizing to her on a daily basis, which had since dropped down to a weekly phone call. Their relationship was under repair, but she'd gotten tired of living in the past. Sometimes, it felt like he used her as a crutch, and she needed him to stand on his own.

Braylin rolled her shoulders, sending thoughts of Roger away. At least the rest of the maintenance crew had stopped treating her like the enemy after they'd heard about her heroics at the hangar. Not that she felt like a hero. She'd only done what she could to protect herself and Blaze.

Though, she had to admit, sending bad men to jail did feel pretty damned good.

A snarky grin lit Braylin's face, and she turned up the volume on the radio. With her, Blaze, and Roger's testimonies, they'd sent Mr. Arnaud's men to prison. Today marked one month since the trial.

Another reason to celebrate.

Braylin hummed along, sorely out of tune, while she thought about the fact that today also marked six months since she'd first met Blaze.

It alternately felt like forever and no time at

all. Their relationship was easy in the best possible way. He made her feel loved, cherished . . . *whole*. No more building walls for protection. With him, she didn't need them.

For the first time in a long time, she felt like herself—the person she'd been before Rob.

Blaze had given her that, and she would spend the rest of her days showing him how grateful she felt. That's why she planned to make this anniversary one he would never forget.

* * *

Blaze needed a shower. He had ash on top of dirt on top of a layer of he didn't want to know what. The blonde hairs on his arms didn't catch the glow of the light cast by the setting sun. They were practically black. He tugged his sleeves down to cover them as he climbed the stairs to Braylin's apartment.

He and his crewmates had fought against a fire until the bitter end of the season. He'd been digging line and mopping up for too many days straight, bleeding into too many nights. When he'd slept, it had been in the open without the luxury of even a tent, much less a shower. But none of that mattered because he was almost home, and Braylin waited for him.

A smile pulled the corners of his mouth up as he trailed a hand along the wooden railing. She lived on the top floor of the three-story apartment building. It was a newer build with pretty blue-gray boards crowning a first-story stacked-stone façade. Timber-framed trusses stained a bright maple decorated the walkways between units, adding to the faux rustic feel.

He'd practically lived there since he'd told Braylin he loved her. He hadn't been back to California in months. It seemed eons as well as miles away, but a part of him wanted to take her there. To show her where he grew up and where his love of the outdoors began. Maybe after he proposed . . .

The question desperately wanted to leap from his lips, but he hadn't even bought a ring yet. He shook his head as he reached the landing. He would soon, though. Once he found one that matched the beauty of his angel, he'd ask her to make him the luckiest man alive.

A skitter of nervous energy tensed his shoulders. He felt pretty sure she'd say yes, and if she didn't . . . he'd do his damnedest to convince her otherwise. No more walking away. Not from her.

Reaching the door to her apartment, Blaze

fished the key out of his pocket. The sight of his hands made him sigh. He'd washed them, yet somehow, they were still covered in smudges. Soot marked his skin, but underneath, ash and dirt had taken up permanent residence within the cracks and calluses on his palms. Wiping them on his pants only made the marks worse. If he looked this bad, he didn't want to think about how he smelled. He'd have to warn Braylin and head straight for the shower.

His stomach tightened in anticipation as he reached for the doorknob. He put his key in but found it already unlocked. Thinking Braylin had left it that way, expecting his arrival, he pushed open the door. "Honey, I'm home," he trilled with a cocky grin.

Blaze put his hands up, ready to stop Braylin's advance on him, but she didn't immediately appear. He dropped his pack on the hardwood floor of the entryway and winced when it left a black mark against the light-gray painted wall on its way down. His boots followed, knowing better than to track them across the pale carpet. He grimaced at his socks; the cream had turned into a splotchy gray. Pulling them off, he then inspected his feet. At least *they* were clean.

"Braylin?" he called out and waited for a

response. When he didn't get one, his heart skipped a beat before hammering against his rib cage.

They hadn't had any trouble since their showdown with Mr. Arnaud's men in court, but what if . . . Blaze swallowed hard. He didn't need to jump to conclusions, especially ones that made him break out in fear sweats.

But his body wasn't listening to his brain. His feet rushed down the hall to her bedroom, desperate to find her. That's when he heard it— the shower. Relief settled his pulse.

She's safe.

Taking a deep, calming breath, he walked to the ensuite. Steam floated out the open bathroom door, and Blaze paused on the threshold. The shower stall's glass sides had become opaque with condensation, but the back of it remained open. The opening faced the door, and he'd been struck dumb by the sight of water raining down Braylin's body. Out of all his fantasies of her—and he had a lot—this one recurred the most.

So damn gorgeous. And all mine.

His dick strained his zipper as he watched her lean into the spray with her eyes closed. A soft smile graced her lips, and he wondered if she thought of him. When she turned to rinse the suds out of her milk chocolate hair, he got a view of her delectable backside. She had the juiciest peach he'd ever seen.

He had to get his hands on it.

Two weeks suddenly seemed like an eternity, and Blaze ripped at his clothes. He needed to be in that shower with her like he needed air to breathe. When he'd rid himself of his dingy garments, he walked right in.

Braylin faced away from him with her head tilted under the path of the water. His arms came around her middle, and she jumped, letting out a gasp. He chuckled, and she instantly relaxed at the sound.

Dipping his head, he dropped a kiss on her shoulder before whispering in her ear, "Miss me?"

She leaned back, and that sweet ass of hers brushed against his very erect length. "I should say no just for scaring me like that."

But when he gazed down into her face, her eyes glowed gold with happiness, making him smile. "I sure as hell missed *you*."

A mischievous grin danced across her pretty face. "Prove it."

Hot damn. He'd be happy to.

Blaze turned her and lifted his arms to cup her face. Holding her still felt like a dream. He didn't know what he'd done to deserve her, but he thanked the universe every damned day for it. Brushing his thumbs across her cheeks, he bent his head for a kiss.

Braylin stopped him with a laugh. "What did you do? Fall in the ash?" She stroked his forearms, and her hands came away black.

Shit. He'd forgotten about that. First, from worry over her safety, then the sight of a naked Braylin tended to send most other thoughts scattering from his head. "Sorry. Maybe let me rinse off, then I'll prove how much I missed you." He winked and reached for the bar of soap, but Braylin took it from him.

With a saucy stare, she purred, "Let me."

Blaze couldn't say no to her if he wanted to; she owned every piece of him. Emotions bubbled up, choking in their intensity, and he forced them down. "Sure thing, little lady," he drawled in the fakest country accent he could muster.

She shook her head, but he glimpsed the smile she tried to hide. "You're *so* funny."

She'd dragged out the 'so' for effect, mocking him, and he grinned ferally, thinking he'd have to give her a spank for that later. As she gently soaped his arms, his hands clenched against the desire to grab ahold of her, bend her over, and drive himself home.

Two damn weeks.

He blinked and found her watching him with a knowing smile. "Not in a hurry, are we?"

Braylin washed him in slow, teasing circles. Up his arms and onto his chest before traveling lower. His cock twitched in anticipation, but she swabbed his legs instead.

On a pained chuckle, he told her, "Woman, you're a horrible tease."

The look she gave him in response was pure delight. She knew what she did to him and loved every minute of it. She took her time with the creases at his hips. Long enough that his blood roared in his head by the time she moved on. When she knelt in front of him, his hips jerked involuntarily.

She bent her head with a grin and licked up his length. More torture, but damned if he didn't love it. When her lips closed around his tip, his hand slapped the tiles. She sucked him in, and he groaned. "Fuck, that's amazing."

In response, she pulled him deeper, humming in her throat, and he felt the vibration all the way to his bones. The soap bar dropped with a wet thud; then, her hand joined her mouth.

"Braylin." It had been too long, and what she

was doing felt too damned good. He had to stop her, or he was going to blow. "Angel, stop," Blaze rasped.

She made a noise of protest, making his eyes nearly roll back in his head. "Angel," came out in a growl this time, and he reached for her hair to hold her still. When she met his eyes, he demanded, "Stop. I want to come inside you."

She released him with a disappointed sigh, but he pulled her up, capturing that amazing mouth with his own. She tasted like his, like he'd already claimed her, and love filled his chest with a warmth so strong it made him dizzy. He freed her lips and dropped his forehead to hers. "I love you, Braylin."

He felt, more than saw, her mouth curve in reply. "I love you too."

Blaze leaned back and stared into her hazel eyes. Gold dominated now; it had become his favorite to glimpse in them. As he stared, he thought he could spend hours deciphering their colors and never grow bored.

My angel.

Her hand closed around his length, and his blood traveled south, ratcheting up his pulse.

"Didn't you have something to prove?" she teased as she squeezed.

A grin creased his face. Then he spun her around, lifting her hands to splay them against the tile wall. Leaning down, he found the spot behind her ear that made her moan. "I do, don't I?"

He stepped back to admire her curves before caressing all that soft skin, slick with water droplets. Starting with her arms, he trailed his hands down to her breasts, teasing her like she'd teased him. First massaging, then pinching until she whimpered, and he knew what she wanted, what she needed.

Gripping that delicious rear end, Blaze bent Braylin over and sheathed himself.

"Mmm, yesss." She rocked back, urging him on.

With one palm braced on the wall, he pulled her flesh to his until they were flush—her back to his front. Tight and deep, her body welcomed him as he delved into her, hips pumping.

No matter how many times they made love, he never stopped wanting her.

Now, he relished the feel of her closing around his length as he drove them both to oblivion. His heart and his lungs rushed toward release, but he held on until he could take her with him.

His hand roamed her curves while her

lavender vanilla scent mixed with the steam and suffused his senses. It added to the pleasure fogging his brain, and he could only think of her. Reaching for the bundle of nerves at her center, he added pressure as he thrust.

"Ohhh—"

"Are you close, angel?" he grunted between rapid breaths.

"Yes! God, Blaze, just like that!" Braylin screamed.

He pumped harder, panting like he'd run a marathon, until he felt her inner muscles clench around him. It snapped the tether on his control. Everything tightened, and with a groan that shook his whole body, the inferno of his release erupted.

Seconds or minutes later, the water coming from the showerhead had grown cold. He reached blindly and slapped it off. Nuzzling into the hair on Braylin's nape, he hummed in satisfaction. Every muscle in his body felt loose, so loose that his tongue wagged of its own accord.

"Marry me, Braylin," he murmured into her skin.

A pause long enough for his head to wake up had Blaze stiffening with regret, but then she spoke, "What did you say?"

This wasn't how he'd meant to ask her. But the

words were out, and he'd meant them. He wanted her and no one else, so he pushed off the wall, turning her to face him.

"Will you marry me?" he rasped, hoping the desperation twisting his gut didn't bleed into his words.

Those gorgeous hazel eyes stared, unblinking. She seemed . . . stunned.

"Angel?" *Please say yes.*

After a moment, she blinked and started to laugh. Blaze's chest squeezed uncomfortably; she thought his proposal was a joke. He backed away to lean against the opposite wall, suddenly cold despite the steam fogging the shower.

But she shook her head and reached for him, wrapping her arms around his neck with a smile. "I was going to ask *you.*"

"What?" His brain must not be firing on all cylinders yet. *Did she mean . . .?* "*You* were going to propose to *me*?"

Braylin nodded and hummed, "Mm-hmm. Tonight. It's our six-month anniversary."

Six months . . . When he realized, Blaze's face lit with his cocky smile. "Since you saved my life?"

Her face softened, and her palm rubbed the scruff on his jaw. "Since we met."

Blaze smirked against the nervous adrenaline

surging in his veins. Thankfully, it didn't crack his voice as he asked, "So, is that a yes, then?"

She raised a brow in response. "Are *you* saying yes?"

He loved this woman, but she delighted in being difficult. He cupped her hips and squeezed. "I asked first."

That got him a pout. "I guess you did beat me to the punch."

"Yep. What's it going to be, angel?" He grabbed a handful of peach and tapped too lightly to be considered a spank before rubbing soothing circles on all that supple flesh. "Want to make me the luckiest man alive?"

She snorted. "I don't know if that's what you get for marrying me, but the answer is . . . yes."

At her glowing smile, warmth ignited in his chest and spread until it filled every single cell to bursting. "My angel wife."

Her golden eyes glinted. "My hotshot husband."

Blaze lowered his head for a kiss to seal the deal. Even though they hadn't made the vows yet, he had no doubt they'd be walking down the aisle very soon. The certainty that Braylin belonged to him and he to her—that he'd found his *home*—was enough to fuel the fire of his love for all the seasons together they had left on this earth.

ACKNOWLEDGMENTS

This book was supposed to be a short story for an anthology, but the more I got into it, the more I realized these characters needed to stand alone. Their story was too important not to. For starters, there aren't enough female veterans in fiction, especially those working in male-dominated industries like aviation. Braylin represents those women and champions the fact they can get the job done—no extra appendage needed!

The other under-represented group in this book is the wildland firefighters, the hotshots—both men and women—who are truly unsung heroes. Working tirelessly in hazardous conditions, these firefighters deserve so much more gratitude than I can give.

If you want to support them, consider donating to the Wildland Firefighter

Foundation. This foundation assists families of fallen and injured firefighters. I don't get anything if you donate. I'm just someone who believes in their mission trying to spread the word.

On that note, I want to thank the entire community of wildland firefighters. Not only for what they do to protect us but for inspiring this book.

And a very big, gigantic, humongous thank you to my husband, who works as an aerial firefighter (i.e., Braylin's job). Thank you for brainstorming with me, inspiring me, and helping me with technical things I didn't (don't) understand. Oh, and for bugging your former hotshot friend with my questions when I needed it ☺

Two other people critical in making this book happen are my amazing critique partners, M.K. and Nina. You two gals are the best Dream Team I could ask for. Thank you for helping make Blaze and Braylin's story a reality.

And thank you to my Shades ladies, whose support means the world. Having you all keeps me sitting in front of the keyboard every day.

Finally, thank *you*—the readers—for buying this book! I hope you enjoyed Blaze and Braylin's adventure and that if you didn't know much about wildland firefighting, it made you want to learn more!

A NOTE TO READERS

If you enjoyed reading this book, please consider leaving me a review. I'd love to know what you liked—about the plot, the characters, or something else—or if you had a favorite scene. Authors are so happy when readers leave reviews because it helps spread the word about our books through the recommendation process and helps new readers decide if our books will be a good fit for them. It also helps with our rankings on sites like Amazon, making our stories more visible to new readers.

If you are interested in my future books, please subscribe to my newsletter. By subscribing, you receive an EXCLUSIVE novella featuring a woman on the run and forced proximity with a troubled military hero! You can also follow me on social media for updates, teasers, and more.

All my links can be found here: https://linktr.ee/blyedonovan.

Thank you for reading!

xoxo,

Blye Donovan

BOOKS BY
BLYE DONOVAN

Rolling Brook Series
Hunted at Whiteford Farm
Gifts from a Stalker
Small Town Frame-up
Condemned by Secrets
Marked as Queen of Hearts

Stand-alone Novels
Undercover Santa
Blaze of Glory

ABOUT THE AUTHOR

Blye Donovan is a military brat and a veteran who resides in the Lowcountry of South Carolina with her husband and fur-child, Max. Besides books, she's addicted to coffee, wine, and shoes. When she's not feeding these addictions, she writes books that are romantic suspense stories featuring strong heroines and alpha protector heroes overcoming dangerous villains. Her books are  set in small towns because she loves the atmosphere associated with them, especially when they have historic architecture. She was supposed to become a historic preservationist, but . . . writing has always been her passion. You can check out her current series, follow her on social media, and more at this link: https://linktr.ee/blyedonovan.